Eat at Zeke's
A family drama.

By Christopher CJX Joseph

Author of 'Road Kill 'Pathfinder'
And 'Road Kill 'Crossroads' *coming soon.*

All available on Amazon Kindle and Barnes and Noble.

Inquires
Christopher.j88@gmail.com

Cover: Courtesy Travers Flynn Photography

Dedications

My 3 gambinos Mykal, Myana & Aryana.

For my mother Carolyn, for her whimsical words of wisdom, artistic virtues, and editing expertise.

For that special someone in my life who encourages me to climb great heights. (Even though I hate heights!)

In honour of my late father Norman 'Zeke' Joseph who always kept on my tail 24/7 and shared with me the joy of homemade ice cream!

Homemade Ice Cream

1¾ cups heavy cream
1¼ cup whole milk
¾ cup sugar
⅛ teaspoon fine sea salt
1 tablespoon vanilla extract or 1 vanilla bean split in half lengthwise
or
Optional: 2 cups of add-ins - soft brownies, cookies, and blondies or whatever you like.

Pour 1 cup of the cream into a saucepan and add the sugar, salt. Scrape the seeds of the vanilla bean into the pot and then add the vanilla pod to the pot. Warm the mixture over medium heat, just until the sugar dissolves. Remove from the heat and add the remaining cream, milk, and vanilla. Stir to combine and chill in the refrigerator.
When ready to churn, remove the vanilla pod, whisk mixture again and pour into ice cream maker. Churn according to the manufacturer's instructions. Transfer the finished ice cream to an airtight container and place in the freezer until ready to serve. Enjoy!

Eat@Zeke's

Recipe Parts:

Eat@Zeke's:

Part I:

Mama's Flour Bed

Southern Cornbread

1-1/2 cups yellow cornmeal
1-1/2 cups general all-purpose flour
4 tablespoons baking powder
2 tablespoons sugar
1 teaspoon salt
1-1/2 cups milk
2 eggs
2 tablespoons vegetable oil
2 tablespoons melted butter

Preheat oven to 375 degrees F (175 degrees C). Grease an 8-inch square pan. Melt butter in large skillet. Remove from heat and stir in sugar. Quickly add eggs and beat until well blended. Combine buttermilk with baking soda and stir into mixture in pan. Stir in cornmeal, flour, and salt until well blended and few lumps remain. Pour batter into the prepared pan.

Bake in the preheated oven for 30 to 40 minutes, or until a toothpick inserted in the center comes out clean.

Detroit. *(Post reconstruction)*

Early morning, a bittersweet chilly spring. The sun rises pink and blue hues through dew covered evergreens, moist heavy grass, pothole laden abandoned streets, and rows of dilapidated houses and business littering the eastside of Detroit, Michigan. Mama Woods drives her Buick cautiously, crossing 7 Mile with its bustling liquor, porn, gun, and pawn shops. Playing soothing jazz, she passes by a closed auto plant with striking workers huddled around a burning trash can in impromptu camps. She honks, waves, supporting familiar faces.

Further, Mama slows to a stop, cautious of young pre-schoolers entering the local community center, where her long-time friend, Freddy Styles, catches her eye as he sweeps the walkway. Entertaining wandering kids, Freddy does the moonwalk and robot dances for their enthusiastic responses before sending them on their way. Mama laughs, for a seventy-year-old man, Freddy still had fresh moves. He sees her and smiles wide, waves.

She passes by a well-kept gas station, already being bum rushed by the early morning drunks. Her middle-eastern friends, brothers Akee and Bama wave at her between fussing at the disorderly and sweeping their entrance.

Mama arrives at a small well-kept diner nestled between a gas station and more abandoned buildings. Mama exits the car, adjusts her simple but classy outfit and pulls her keys out at the back door.

She feels him before she sees him, Pook, her diminutive prep-chef and maintenance man pops up from behind the dumpster startling her.

Pook nonchalantly quips, “Mama, what you doing here so early?”

Mama exhales, “Oh my goodness, boy don't do that! Why are you behind the dumpster?”

He snickers, “Mama you okay? Goodness, you know the grease pit back there! Anyways I thought you were going to take it light, be easy greasy, stroll in whenever? Go home, Mama!”

She sighs and looks over the battered diner, the siding in desperate need of paint, the vegetation creeping up in the jagged cracks of the pavement, replying, “Pooky... this is my home.”

Inside, she turns on the fluorescent sign that blinks slowly before softly illuminating, 'Zeke's Kitchen'. Mama sighs and walks around the diner looking around, eyeing the neatly arranged tables, perfectly placed condiments, the neatly folded menus.

Tanya, one of the waitresses, walks by, smiles, “You're a diehard Mama”. She proceeds to pull down chairs getting ready for their opening. Mama watches as her youngest daughter, Silvia Woods, hurries in, dishevelled, heads for the computer in the diner's office. Mama observes the time as Silvia is busy texting, oblivious to her mother stalking her.

Silvia shifts with ease from texting to opening Facebook on the diner's computer. Mama crosses her arms, taps her foot, glaring at Silvia before clearing her throat, startling her with two simple words, "You're late."

Silvia does a double take, stutters, "Oh uh, Mom, um why aren't you still at home?"

"I'm always up before you, even just taking it easy, I'm still more punctual than you. I really hope you have enough time to squeeze in actual work before you have to be at classes."

"Yes Momma, I understand. I will."

Pook flips on the neon open sign. An eccentric, vagrant looking elderly man, but devoted regular named Tyrone Hill is already in the door, pouncing at Mama as she emerges from the office. Mama thwarts his eager attempt to embrace her. He bemuses, "Mama so blessed the day you are here to grace us with your presence! I do so miss you when you're absent. I trust you have my grits, eggs sunny-side up with just a dab of salt, 2 slices of bacon, toast - buttered both sides, and a glass of O.J. all ready for me boo."

Mama looks at him cross-eyed, mouthed 'Boo?' Rubs her head and pivots behind the counter as customers start to pour in. Shaking her head at Tyrone, "Tyrone you know you can't eat all that stuff; your doctor put you on a strict diet dear, talk to Tanya here, she has you covered with what the doctor prescribed."

Tyrone puffs his chest out, "Mama! 40 years you know what I order - I can't do it - I can't do it! Besides, I'm just following a prime example." Mama narrows her eyes at his added comment. She sighs and leans up against the counter as other regulars attempt to get her attention.

Tanya slides between them, smiling, "I got this Mama." And serves Tyrone his doctor approved healthy meal to expected grunts and groans. The booths and tables are already filled as Mama watches her attentive staff tackle the morning onslaught of devotees and newcomers, she contemplates the future of the diner moving on without her.

She glances to her left, catching the cook, Suga, wiping grease on her apron while eyeing Mama sideways, and hoping she would get away with it. Mama shakes her head in disgust before wincing from a pain in her side as the scent and sizzle of bacon assault her. Tanya is suddenly in front of her, "Mama, you okay? Thought you were semi-retired? You need to go home, sweetie. Take care of those gorgeous flower beds you have."

The door chimes as more customers arrive, Mama is patting Tanya's shoulder, "Thanks dear but I am fine, as I said before and again, this is my home, plus I have flowers here that nobody takes care of. Now go get Mr. Robinson and his daughter Della who just came in, Suga should already have a regular number three and twelve ready for them. Plus tell Della I need three Samoa cookie boxes from her Girl Scouts. Can take it out of the till."

Mama slowly makes her way back to the office where Silvia is chatting on Facebook. She sees Mama and flips the screen to the budget. Mama narrows her eyes at her and notices her potted plants looking dry, she starts to water them and quips as cheerfully as she can, "So how's the budget going? Is the paperwork done? Your class is in about 35 minutes and I don't want you to be late. Was your online buddy giving you proper advice?"

Caught, Silvia blushes, stutters, "Uh, um, well I... Listen, mom, I know what time it is, I'm just about done with it, the good news is we're in the black, and next year looks promising."

Mama adjusts her glasses, eyes her daughter for a moment, making Silvia squirm. She practically snatches a graph, "Did you even budget in the requirements we received from the inspector? This building is fifty years old, do you really think we have the budget for what they want?"

"But mom, I thought that was separate, maybe we can get a small business loan or possibly even talk to Junior...?"

"Child, be real - little Zeke is going to continue investing in here what he has been - nothing - get it out your mind! And no, the banks are not going to invest in this neighborhood after the closing of the auto plant. Don't you notice all this blight around here? What your father and I dreamed about for you kids so long ago is not a concrete reality..."

"Mother I'm sorry but I didn't think..."

"You never think."

Flustered, Silvia scrambles through her paperwork. Mama squints her eyes peering out the office window at a honeybee landing on a petunia in her flower bed. Rays of sunshine illuminate the insect as she takes in every detail of his busy work. Digressing, she puts her hand on Silvia's shoulder, "Baby, I'm sorry, your mother has been under a lot of stress lately with everything going on with the diner and your siblings. The loss of your father still devastates me all these years later."

Silvia puts her hand on her mother's, "Mother, you know I understand. It's okay. You're my mom, by design I'm always there for you."

"I do appreciate it so much, but baby, I do want you to blossom and see the world. There is so much more than between 8 Mile and 7 Mile with closed auto plants, liquor and guns stores, hookers and lottery with abandoned houses carrying filth and disease."

"Mother..."

Mama shushes her before she can continue, and they hold each other tight. Silvia wipes away tears. Mama stands up, "So um, on this book of faces you ever locate your brother?"

"Facebook Mom! It's Facebook, and no, I haven't been able to find Kevin on here, you've asked me this time and time before. He doesn't have an account. Someone not wanting to be found will make sure they can't be found!"

"Well... I don't understand all this techmo gizmo. I heard you can find anybody that's anybody on here. We had to use handwritten letters, stamps, this generation just tap, tap, taps..."

They smile at each other and have an understanding. "Now make sure your figures are correct before you head off to class. Be sure to put that phone away when the teacher is talking, hear me?"

"Yes ma'am." Silvia gets back to the budget as Mama pivots towards the kitchen.

Pleased with herself, Mama repeats, "Tap, tap, taps..."

Silvia snickers, "Mama..."

Again, "Tap, tap, taps..."

Silvia narrows her eyes concerned, "Mama?"

"Tap, tap, taps..." Mama wipes the sweat off her brow, stumbles back a bit. Mama turns around puzzled, upset, looking back at Silvia. "That's what I don't expect from you kids; everything, everything is not what we wished for..."

Silvia mouths out "What…?"

Tanya comes out of the storeroom as Mama twists around and stumbles through the kitchen. Tanya drops the box of towels, "Mama! Are you okay?"

Silvia pushes back her chair as her mother stumbles, "Mom? Mom? What is going on?"

Mama babbles, "They don't care, ungrateful kids, everything we worked for..."

Tanya attempts to assist her up, "Mama what's wrong?"

"Tap, tap, taps..." Mama feels herself out of control, her restaurant spinning around her, everything contorted, shaking, confusing. She is a few paces from the counter as Suga steps around the grill, tries to help Tanya.

Silvia stands quickly, unfortunately she is wrapped up in the computer wires and subsequently knocks over all of the equipment in her haste.

Pook is serving an irate Tyrone who is hoping up and down upset, "I said eggs sunny side up damn it! What is this horse-poop you serving me? I want Mama right now!"

Silvia screams, "MOTHER!!!!"

Pook and Tyrone shut up immediately, look towards the kitchen aghast.

Mama blinks, watches her familiar surroundings grow dim, as if somebody hit a rewind button, she is transported back to the diners grand opening in the sixties, the social unrest of the civil rights movement, strikes at auto plants, the eventual closing of them, the kids growing up and leaving the deteriorating neighborhood, Zeke Sr. passing, to newer struggles such as rebuilding the city, corrupt politicians, the Flint water crisis and all culminating with horrific violence in the street.

Tanya and Suga struggle with Mama as she falls, as she was a cook for forty years, and her shape reflects her long time love for food. The waitresses are no match. Gravity pulls Mama's body free from their grip, her arms take down rows of neatly arranged cookie jars, in single file the jars crash with sickening eruptions as she abruptly twists and hits the floor, face first knocking her helpers backward.

The entire store screams quietly as everybody shares a moment of shock. Silvia drops to her knees, built up aggression emerging, "NOOOOOOOOOO!!!"

The familiar faces soften, blur together brightly as the honeybee in her flower bed. Tanya tries to administer first aid and her baby Silvia sobs uncontrollably, not sure how to help. Tanya cries out, "Somebody call 911! Somebody call 911!"

Tyrone sits down discombobulated, "Sorry Mama, all I wanted was them sunny-side up."

Silvia sobs, caressing her mother's face. Mama manages to touch her, struggling to speak, she murmurs, "Sweetie, you must make your own bed, and lay in it, it'll be okay. It will be okay." She feels the love in the room as she gazes out at the honeybee slowly taking the nectar.

Eat@Zeke's

Part.II:

The Big Fish

Grilled Salmon

6 salmon fillets, without skin (about 4 ounces each)
1 tablespoon minced garlic
⅓ brown sugar
3 teaspoons parsley, flakes
6 teaspoons butter
1 large lemon, squeezed and juiced
vegetable spray

Season salmon fillets with lemon pepper, garlic powder, and salt. In a small bowl, stir together soy sauce, brown sugar, water, and vegetable oil until sugar is dissolved. Place fish in a large re-sealable plastic bag with the soy sauce mixture, seal, and turn to coat. Refrigerate for at least 2 hours.

Preheat grill for medium heat. Lightly oil grill grate. Place salmon on the preheated grill, and discard marinade. Cook salmon for 6 to 8 minutes per side, or until the fish flakes easily with a fork.

Dallas

Ezekiel Woods commands the Dallas meeting room full of men in suits, his arms, and hands orchestrating a symphony captivating the skeptical crowd. The harem of suits nods their heads in unison as he pours over data, overhead charts, graphs, statistical analysis, and numerical formulas. He wins their approval as his eyes gaze across the lone female clapping along. Ezekiel smiles and winks at her as she blushes.

His assistant Ms. Kane interrupts the meeting, "I'm sorry, Mr. Woods, you have an urgent call."

"Ms. Kane, sorry is not an excuse, we are conducting important..."

"Mr. Woods, it's your family, something happened."

Ezekiel pauses, looks over the room and at his business partner Marty Simon who nods okay. Ezekiel checks his cell, 22 missed calls, he grimaces, answers the next call as the suits murmur among themselves. Marty eyes his partner as Ezekiel's facial expressions turns from disbelief to sorrow.

"Gentlemen, and a lady." He glances over at the female partner, "Final offer is on the table for Digizoic Industries, fifty-two dollars a share, the assets portfolio is being passed out to you now by my assistant. My apologies but I have to cut my time short, my partner Mr. Simon will fill you in additional detail, I trust you'll come to the right conclusion."

Ezekiel gathers everything quickly into his attaché case, dons his Brooks Brothers jacket and rushes out the door as Marty struggles to keep up. Marty starts to speak but is cut short, "My mother just got rushed to the hospital, I have to go back to Detroit. You got this."

Marty gasps, "Whatever you need partner."

Ms. Kane looks over at them talking, he pauses, finishes with Marty.

"I need you to close, do it."

Marty nods okay as he peers into the room of suits hesitantly. Ms. Kane watches intensely as Ezekiel speed walks out of the building.

Detroit

Ezekiel exits the airline terminal as his wife Kayla awaits. She stands and takes his carry on, looking into his face, "I'm so sorry."

He sucks his lips, eyes her for a moment before answering a call on his Bluetooth, "No fifty-two is the lowest we'll go..." Kayla falls in line behind him, trailing as he talks business through the terminal.

He continues talking business getting into his black BMW 7-Series. He's still conversing as he merges onto I-75 north, stuck in the five-o'clock rush hour. Kayla watches his hands move, orchestrating deals worldwide. She wonders if he could get away with that behaviour debating a drug deal on Detroit's east side. She smirks at the thought of him floating belly up in Lake Ontario.

Ezekiel storms into the hospital with Kayla stumbling behind him trying to catch up. He continues his conversation, "Mortimer you want me to move 200 shares of Apple to Chrysler for what? You think they're dropping the next big iCar or something?" He summons a nurse, "Tyla Woods room please," She points down the hallway. Barely pausing for his conversation, "So what is this - a hunch? I don't think so! You screw me over I'm taking back that 100k portfolio I helped you earn for your botched investments - comprehend?"

Hospital staff hops out of his way as he bulldozes past a no cell phone sign. Doctor Sharon walks out of Mama's room looking over her paperwork.

He puts away the phone and is in her face. "Doctor - give me a prognosis - I need to know what's happening with my mother *right now*."

She pauses, studies him, bemused, "Okay, and you are?"

"Excuse me? I'm her son! You want a subpoena..."

"Oh, are you Kevin?"

Ezekiel almost collapses as Kayla leans forward, "This is Mrs. Woods oldest son - Ezekiel Woods Jr., of the law firm Simon - Woods - Simon - yeah, not the younger brother, you might want to fill him in now".

"The younger, missing-in-action, running from the law, idiot brother - mind you."

Dr. Sharon looks back and forth between them, realizing her situation, she huffs, “I see.” She pauses and looks over at Tanya flanked by the elderly Vergeman sisters, lifelong friends of Mama's in the waiting room who nod their acknowledgment. The obvious tension between them and Ezekiel fills the room as they frown at his arrival. Nonetheless they wouldn’t stand in the way of Tyla and her son. Ezekiel ignores their disapproval, shrugging them off as two old evil hags who cake on too much makeup, and hover around his mother like bats.

The doctor continues, “Sorry, she had asked about a Kevin. Okay, Mr. Woods, I will be straight with you, your mother has had a severe cardiac arrest, she is stabilized now but she is not out of the woods yet.”

Ezekiel exhales, "Are you attempting humor?”

“No pun intended."

“I don't want any interns treating my mother, you hear me? Shouldn't have brought her to the community hospital! I'm going in.”

“Wait…sir!”

Ezekiel barges into his mothers' room still checking his Blackberry. Silvia is curled up in a chair, her face and hair caked with tears. She sees him and leaps attempting to hug him, which turns into an awkward moment, as Ezekiel is unsure how to hug back. He clears his throat, "Do you need any money?"

Silvia eyes him confused, shakes her head, "What?"

Ezekiel, "I said did you need money, anything? I realize you are still an idler dependent on mother for your daily needs..."

"Wait, what? Thanks for the insult you insensitive jerk! No big brother, I work, I go to school, and I'm just fine without your crappy money! How about you stop slacking and see how your mother is doing? Sheesh!" She storms off in a huff, mumbling under her breath as Ezekiel looks at her flabbergasted, not sure what he said wrong. From the hallway, Kayla looks at him disappointingly. He shrugs and turns to his mother.

He looks over the intervening tubes going into her veins, her slow but steady heartbeat pulsing through the equipment. He takes a hard breath, not certain how to deal with seeing his mother like this. He sees moisture around her face and takes a handkerchief to wipe it off. The compassion throws him off guard, Ezekiel feels his head swell and he sits next to his mother. He takes her hand and caresses it softly, feeling his own face getting moist.

Kayla watches in shock, having to sit down herself, not sure how to handle his surprising actions.

Zeke's Kitchen

At the diner, the staff walks around the store in slow motion, placid, transfixed, not sure what to do next. An elderly man, Freddy Styles slim, fit, walks in with a coach's uniform on, followed by a group of youth baseball players. Pook is counting down the register, "Pook, Pook, I heard what was happening! How is Mama doing?"

Pook jabs away at the register, frustrated, saddened, he stares into space, "I can still see her here laying on the floor Freddy. It's not looking good man"

Tyrone exaggerates, "It's the big one Elizabeth, I'm coming, it's the big one - Elizabeth!"

Freddy and Pook look over, then back, Freddy shakes his head. "Uh, yeah anyways, we left the game early, so I could go see her. I told the boy's parents to pick them up here."

Pook nods, "Oh yeah, Freddy, you good, go on! They can be here, I can handle them!"

"You sure Pooky - I don't want to put you in an uncomfortable situation!"

"Man, we almost closed now, and this has been one hell of a day, some kids probably brighten up the situation for real. Long as they act okay."

Ezekiel and Kayla walk into the diner, looking around the place disgustingly. She nervously holds onto him tightly.

Pook greets them, “Grab a seat, I'll be right with you.” He turns to Fred, “For real Fred, go on, see Mama.”

“Appreciate it buddy, I will see you.” Freddy turns to the kids, “Boys, we'll resume Thursday - you know how to act in here. I expect a good report from my boy Pooky here.”

Freddy exits as Pook helps the lone waitress Moco, juggle remaining customers. Pook looks at the boys milling around, “Okay, you kids either need to coordinate or evacuate - come on now - you all taking up space!”

A player goes to Moco's aid as she almost drops a tray. They instantly mobilize clearing tables, sweeping floors, bringing out water as Pook looks on impressed. Freddy has taught them well.

Pook eyes Ezekiel and Kayla, “Excuse me, eating or leaving, what’s it gonna be. We bout to close.”

Ezekiel arches his eyebrow, looking down at Pook, “Excuse me?”

“No loitering buddy, snap crackle, we bout to close. Make it pop.”

"Excuse me, colourful man of words, this is a lawsuit waiting to happen, why are underage children working here?'

“All due respect sir, plainly nonya business - need to step - NEXT?”

Tyrone steps towards Ezekiel, "Step aside young blood step aside - before I bust a cap in you!"

Ezekiel narrows his eyes, confused by the elderly man speaking slang, acting belligerent, this was not normal to him. Kayla is practically knocked over as people get takeout and leave. Two players suddenly run into each other crashing drinks everywhere. Ezekiel protests, "Sir I'll have to insist you desist using these children immediately!"

"Excuse me? And who are you - Mr. Knock off Brooks Brothers wearing, fake Rolex wanna be - this ain't the day to play - miss me with that mess!"

Freddy swings back in to grab his coat and sees who Pook is rudely talking to, he rushes over to intervene, "Hey Pook, Pook - chill my man, bro in the *real* Brooks Brother suit, the one looking very impisserated right now - pray to God things don't go bad, maybe your new boss." He lets that sink in before turning to Ezekiel, "Hey Junior - long-time no see - how are you?"

Ezekiel calms down some, "I'm good, thanks, I'm Ezeki..." "

"I know who you are, the eldest of the Woods clan - A founding member of Simon Woods Simon, won that big case for the entire Wolverines rowing team - done some good things. Sr. would be very proud. Surprised you don't remember me, played on my tee-ball league so many years ago."

Pook and Tyrone mouths drop in shock. Ezekiel goes blank, "Um, Mr. um..."

"...Styles."

Ezekiel thinks hard, "Oh! Right, right - Freddy Styles - I remember you! Used to think you were a superman or something - coaching kids, running the community center, teaching at the city college, making films... Oh, and had that Detroit Swag and wearing purple Zoot suits and Gators!"

Tyrone gasps, "Little Zeke? My, these young'n grow up too fast! Damn o'man, and I was doing my best Ice Cube impression - The G you love to hate!"

Freddy snickers, "Oh snap, you remember the suit huh? I believe I still possess it somewhere. You're too kind; I'm retired from a few of those things but yes, that is I. Sorry that this wasn't under better circumstances."

"Thanks, Freddy, I do appreciate it."

Freddy pats Ezekiel's back, "Seems like yesterday that terrible tragedy happened with your pops, did they ever figure out what happened? It's been so long. They clear lil' bro?"

"It's been awhile - nothing new though, nothing new. Don't know about him. Thanks for asking though."

"You been to the hospital yet?"

"Yeah, just got back."

"I'm on my way now."

They both notice a picture on the wall of Zeke Sr., they look at each other and nod.

"I need to go too, been a long day. Just wanted to see the old place." Ezekiel turns to Pook. "Next time no kids working and let's see this place cleaned up okay? Got important people stopping by."

The statement lingers in awkward silence as the surprise guests exit.

Outside, chess tables align the patio, several of the baseball players have pulled out checkers. Ezekiel shakes his head, "Boys, boys, wrong! Wrong! These tables were meant for greatness, intelligent games. Not simple people activities. Need to expand your mind." The boys look at him puzzled. He reaches behind a wall and finds the box of chess pieces. He replaces their game. "Learn, respect, challenge yourselves. Come back and see me when you're of age." The boys look at the chess pieces in shock as Kayla peers questionably at her husband. The couple strolls away confidently.

“Is that where you expanded your mind?” Kayla asks quietly as Ezekiel grunts.

They arrive at their BMW as a limo pulls up blocking them in. Ezekiel motions to her to get in as he approaches the limo cautiously. The back-window slides down, he groans seeing who it is, "Lydell, Lydell Winkelman...you have a knack showing up at the most improper tune times. How can I help you?"

Lydell blows smoke from an electric cigar out the window, "Ezekiel Woods Jr. What a pleasure to see you back in the hood."

"Lydell, what do you want?"

"Not even a hello, greetings, bonjour, hola? Tsk tsk, always such the bourgeois lawyer, cold and impersonal, just like a captain of a debate team that loses... oh wait, is one and the same."

Ezekiel snickers, "Still bringing up old stuff. Listen I have more important things to do. Good day, Winkelman." Ezekiel takes a few steps away.

"Oh, I'm sure. I did hear about your mother; such a tragedy as an abandoned old lady still hangs on to the beloved old restaurant that her offspring care *so little about.* Wasn't even here to comfort her during her time of need."

"I said good day Lydell, don't let me ask again." Ezekiel goes to his car.

"Au contraire my friend, don't forget the agreement we have when this place folds, written in blood. Was just waiting for the old hag to croak. Lord knows her offspring want nothing to do with it!"

Ezekiel slams his car door making Kayla jump. He pulls a baseball bat out of his car, "LIE-dell, that's my MOTHER, sir! And that agreement is not valid, and you know it - if you attempt to challenge me on this - trust and believe - you will be entering a fight you have no chance of winning. Try me! Now better get that light fixed or Detroit's finest will find you!"

"What light?"

Ezekiel swings the bat busting the limo's tail light, "That one! Now move!"

Ezekiel gets back in his car as Kayla's eyes him nervously, "Dear - what was that all about? Who was that?"

"A small-time thug who believes he's bigger than he is."

"I don't like you messing around with..."

"Kay, I'm a grown man, stay out of grown men business okay? Thought we had discussed this?" Ezekiel guns the Beamer and backs up inches from the limo, taunting them to move, Lydell glares back, blowing smoke.

Kayla sucks her lips loudly, "Just, I..."

"Seriously! I can take care of myself okay, I know what I'm doing!"

"You don't help your situation much, do you? You know nothing has changed."

"Tell me something I don't know."

Lydell motions to his driver, closing his window before they speed off. Ezekiel backs up crunching the broken tail light before driving off silently.

Eat@Zekes

Part III:

Pook's BBQ Joint

Grilled Kabob Chicken Recipe

1/2 cup soy sauce
1/2 cup water
1 tablespoon honey
1 tablespoon vegetable oil
2 teaspoon ground mustard
4 boneless skinless chicken breast halves
2 medium zucchinis, cut in 1-1/2-inch slices
1 medium onion, cut in wedges
1 medium green pepper, cut into inch chunks
1/2 small pineapple, cut into wedges

In a large bowl, whisk together oil, honey, soy sauce, and pepper. Before adding chicken, reserve a small amount of marinade to brush onto kabobs while cooking. Place the chicken, garlic, onions and peppers in the bowl, and marinate in the refrigerator at least 2 hours. Preheat the grill for high heat.

Drain marinade from the chicken and vegetables, and discard marinade. Thread chicken and vegetables alternately onto the skewers. Lightly oil the grill grate. Place the skewers on the grill. Cook for 12 to 15 minutes, until chicken juices run clear. Turn and brush with reserved marinade frequently.

Detroit

The setting sun casts shadows over the sparse businesses remaining open on the block as they prepare to close for the night. The front lights go off in Zeke's as the neon closed sign flicks on.

A strong breeze pushes trees sideways, in the darkening light, it casts odd shadows over the back-parking lot of Zeke's Kitchen as Pook navigates his way to the dumpster carrying trash bags. Pook looks around to make sure he's alone and slips out a rolled-up cigarette. Fumbling with his lighter in the wind he ducks behind the fence around the dumpster to achieve lighting it. Inhaling, he breathes deeply reminiscing over the tribulations of the day.

He exhales, blowing smoke towards a partly burned out abandoned duplex directly behind the restaurant. Closing his eyes, he remembers carrying food on a weekly basis to the poor families that used to live there. Freddy and Mama had paired up to help feed many of them living in the area and Pook was often their delivery man.

There had been quite a few children living there and they blamed one of them for starting the fire by playing with a lighter. Never mind the fact that the lighter was discarded by a well-known local drug head who frightened the children sleeping behind the storage shed. No one was exactly sure who dropped the lighter, but theorists including himself suspected foul play because of the fast burning nature of the fire. The duplex shot up like a timber box barely giving the residents time to escape. Weird burn patterns were labelled suspicious, but the arson investigation hit a roadblock when they could not identify an agreeable accelerator, the case ended up unresolved.

Mama's brother, Leon Sullex, was visiting from Ohio at the restaurant. He threw down his fried chicken to race over to the building and was able to yank a trapped mother and her daughter out of a basement window. He was labelled a hero even though he suffered second-degree burns over 55% of his body and inhaled nasty exhaust fumes. He was the real victim of the tragedy as many of the neighborhood residents had just stood and gawked, he put his life on the line.

Leon survived but suffered in recovery, preceding Ezekiel Sr. in death. A year later he passed away quietly in his sleep back home in Yellow Springs. As Detroit kept wrestling with the M.I.A. owner to tear the place down, Mama suffered in silence with the daily reminder of her brother's demise, the burned building, sitting directly behind her parking lot.

"Boy bye! You know you busted! If Mama knew you were sneaking one!"

Pook jumps as the waitress Moco appears behind him. He smiles; taking in her shapely figure, her light skinned caramel features - hence the name - the youngest, prettiest waitress employed at Zeke's. Pook couldn't help having a crush, despite her football-playing boyfriend, and being 15 years younger. "It's all good, I need it for my stress. Keep this between you and me and I won't tell what I know about you!"

"What, what you mean? What you know about me? You don't know nothin'!"

She calls his bluff, Pook just had to throw a crooked smile, "I just saying sweetie, I may know a lil' something, something."

"Yeah right, I hear you Pook! You know you sneaking cause Mama's not here! Anyways, those death sticks do nothing but enhance your stress. Thought you knew! Good night, enjoy!"

He enjoys her backside as she saunters away, "Hey wait, let me walk you!"

"Pook, I'm a big girl, I can take care of myself silly!"

"You know how rough these Motown streets are!"

"And you don't think I'm not packing silly? Thought you knew! My daddy taught me well."

"Yeah, city cops would be pro carry for protection huh," Pook says silently, feeling at a slight disadvantage.

They make it to her tricked out Mustang. She smiles, "Thanks anyway, sweetie. Let's pray for Mama, okay?"

He nods, "Of course, be safe." He waves as she revs up the Stang, bumping bass thumping R&B from Charles Carpenter before pulling out into the night traffic.

He sighs and pivots back to finish throwing the bags away and his cigarette. Something rustles in the swaying brush prompting Pook to drop ash and gets burnt, "Ouch! Son of a..."

The dusk light patterns play with his eyesight as the moonlight emerging engages in a battle with them. An object moves in a broken-out window, sending glass cascading onto ragged cement blocks. Startled, Pook jumps and reaches behind the dumpster for a crowbar that they use to prop the dumpster open. The bush rustles again, he wipes sweat from his brow and yells, "Hey fool, don't mess with me! I may be little, but I got hands of steel!"

He flicks the burning cigarette towards the bush. The embers sparkle and make impact. A black cat suddenly leaps upwards yowling and hissing loudly before scurrying off quickly into the emerging night. Pook yelps and swings the bar, "Holy crap! What the h...!"

He pants, feeling the hair on the back of his neck stand at alert, sending Goosebumps all over his skin. He relaxes, "Damn man, I'm out here acting like a little b..."

A stick crunches in the brush prompting him to step backward. An unseen bird screeches above him as he flinches and follows its path into the moonlight. A cool breeze whips up debris. He lowers his head to catch what looks like a man standing between the bushes. He squints, peering closer at the odd silhouette when the figure suddenly walks briskly towards him.

Pook steps backward and slips, "Hey! Hey! What!"

A man wearing a turban makes crackly noises as he holds what looks like an inscribed box, "A-ca, ca, ca, ca!"

Pook screams and heaves the remaining bag of trash directly at the man's face, it explodes on impact making the man flip backward. He kicks at the squirming, groaning man under the trash and races off shrieking through the parking lot.

Lights engulf him as he skids to a halt in his tracks. He squints, blinded by the light. "Pook, you screaming like a bitch!" He hears hands clapping followed by an uproar of laughter. Flabbergasted and exhausted he drops to his knees, as a group of people emerge in front of their car. "Way to go my man! Took down your attacker with a sack of litter! Showed him whose boss!"

From the pavement, Pook glares up at clean pressed trendy jeans, to an even more primped polo shirt, right up Quentin Jones nostrils as the laughter continues.

"Good job Pooky, you took down a crazy terrorist with nasty leftovers! Didn't see that one coming!" Looking over, Pook sees its Utopia Vergeman, the Vergeman sister's granddaughter with one of her girlfriends from college.

Rounding out the group is Big Moe and Zach, the funky Caucasian of the crew with his sagging skinny jeans and Coogi Jacket. Zach was often considered an Eminem wannabe but vehemently denies that allegation, even though when he freestyles he sounds just like the famous rapper, plus he lives in a trailer park.

Zach offers Pook a hand as Big Moe swipes debris off of Akee Ackbar, the alleged trash terrorist, before assisting him upright.

Akee mumbles as he wipes off something moist, "My head is throbbing, I believe I was blindsided by frozen fish! Pooky, my friend, why you club me with Tilapia?! I thought we were cool, best buddies!"

"Bro, don't ever freak me out like that again, damn!"

"Pooky my friend, Que put me up to it. Que, you owe me fresh new Fila suit, this smells of fish and coffee grounds!" The girls groan as Akee attempts to wipe off filth, usually dressed to impress, the immigrant tries hard to fit in.

Que laughs, "In your dreams Pakistan! You went along with it!"

The store's porch light comes on bathing them in light, the group squints to see Tyrone glaring at them from the kitchen door. He looks them all up and down before his eyes go big staring at Akee, "What the hell happened to you boy? You stink!"

Akee whines, "Pooky pelted me with filth!"

Tyrone cuts him off, "I don't give a what-what! Boy, you bring the beer?!"

Que laughs and holds up a case, "Got it ol' man, let us in!"

"That's what I want to hear, you may enter!"

Pook opens the door as he gives the boys a pound, "You guys did hear what happened to Mama right? The mood is a lil' off playa." Quentin nods as Akee stumbles to the restroom.

Utopia gives Pook a hug, "I know sweetie, I was up there earlier with my grannies. I'm so scared."

Quentin cracks open a brew, "Hey, this is for Mama, we all love her!" He pours the drink into the bush, "She would want us to celebrate her life!"

Zach snickers, "Homie, she doesn't even know we come here after hours!"

"You act like she's already dead Que!" Pook responds as he finishes cleaning the floor.

"Don't waste all that fine drink young man!" Tyrone huffs as he cracks open a cold one.

"Pook, bro, you know we love Mama. She looked out for me since, I was what, yay high?" He extends his palm by his knee. "Mama and Uncle Zeke really helped keep a bro in check, I would have been doing some dumb junk you know what I mean? I really didn't appreciate it back then how they would push me to be in school, and a dummy like me graduated! So, look at me now, I'm getting paper!"

Pook nods in agreement at the same time noticing another young man leaning up against the wall. With the lights out in dining room, he is partially hidden in the shadows with a hoody on and sagging jeans over his Timberlands. He quietly fondles a pack of zigzags. Pook squints, "Hey, you all messing with me again? Who's that?"

Tyrone pops his beer down, "Aww snap, I'm bout to jack a young..."

"Pops chill, that's my man Jaquan, he cool!" Que steps in their way as Jaquan looks on nonchalantly flipping his pack.

"Wait, I knows you! That's that young fool that almost popped Mama! I'mma bout to rock his world yo!" Tyrone grabs his cane.

Pook moves further, "Oh my God, that is him! His picture was up on the wall! You got some nerve son, get stepping!" Big Moe and Zach come forward, not sure which side to support.

"Yo B, it's cool, I'll bounce." Jaquan starts to leave.

Quentin pleads, "Guy, guys, really, it's cool, Mama would vouch for him, how you think he got out of jail?" Jaquan glares defiantly.

Utopia grabs Pook's arm and looks into his eyes, "It's true Pook, Mama bailed him out after he tried to rob the restaurant. She's known him since he was young, really, it's cool. She would want this." Her eyes plead with him as he looks back to Jaquan, then her. Tyrone still tries to move forward as Quentin keeps in his way. Jaquan relaxes, shifts his feet and looks down at the floor. They eye each other for a moment as Pook decides what to do.

Jaquan speaks up, "Look yo, Mama did bail a nig..."

Pook cuts him off, "Hey if you know Mama she doesn't allow that negative word in her restaurant, respect."

Jaquan looks at him puzzled as Tyrone fills him in, "The N-word you dummy! Didn't your mother ever teach you manners?"

"Look, Mama looked out for a-uh, bro, I could have done some time, but she came through ya' knows? She knew life was screwed up for me man, maybe just need a lil' mo' time be like ol' Q here, fo'sho."

Utopia grins and bites her lip gazing at Pook, "Pooky, really, Mama, Freddy, Uncle Zeke, they really looked out for us here like people supposed to you know? I wouldn't be here either, after having my baby boy in school, my Grannies were done with me. Mama insisted I stay in and helped me take care of little Milo, without her, I wouldn't have graduated and been starting college at Wilberforce University next year, yay! I'm in debt to her."

Zach steps forward, "Shoot, I was just white trash at the trailer park. Que and Jaquan here beat my ass every day, stole on a bro, you know! But Mama saw potential in my sketches, got me involved with an arts program at the community center, I'm about to show my work next month!"

Akee re-joins them washed up. Pook eyes him oddly, "Ayo, and stop calling me Pooky! It's Pook!" Akee looks at him and shrugs. Pook sighs. "Hey, is that my shirt?"

"You slime me with trash Pooky, I took the shirt, you owe me!"

Pook reaches for his shirt, "Hey fool, did you wear deodorant with it!"

Akee slides behind the girls, "Pook my friend, back off! You know Akee wears the good stuff!"

He bats Pook's hand off as the girls laugh and intervene. "Pook, I too was a reject in the hood when we arrive after 9.11 to open gas station in dying city, I know all of you had stereotypes and prejudices when my fam and I arrived, just like we had of you. Mama was the first to extend the fig leaf, cooked me and my brother good plates of greens, squash, succulent potatoes with spicy mac and cheese, the juicy meat we weren't even supposed to eat. And yo kid, we were hooked! Once you go black you don't go back! We are brothers, we found a home here, we are proud to know Mama, her spirit is pure. This right here, all of us together, this is the true essence of the America we know and appreciate." The girls clap their hands.

Moe licks his lips, "Akee makes Moe hungry." They look at him and roll their eyes, "Really, that sounds good, you want a confession? Mama save Moe with her cooking! Beefed Big Moe up with the good stuff. Look at me now - bulked up- Moe plays football for the minor league! Where's the food Pook?!"

"You knows, that big idiot has a point, it's time to eat and drink!" Tyrone grunts.

Utopia's friend clears her throat as they take her in, not noticing her until now, a petite blonde standing out in a party dress, "Wow, I'm jealous. I never had the privilege to know Mama like all of you, she sounds wonderful. Maybe that's why Utopia really looked out for me at our school when I had some problems."

"It's in her blood miss." Tyrone points out as Pook nudges him.

"You can call me Sasha." They all greet her warmly.

"Well, ladies and gents, it looks like the tribe has spoken. We've all been touched one way or another by Mama and the Woods love. She gave me a chance right out of serving some time many years ago. I got hip to her and Zeke after graduating from a Re-Entry program and got my life straight from there. Been here ever since." He gives a nod to Jaquan. "She's really shined bright on this hodgepodge family here and this neighborhood. She ok'd it, we're okay with it, welcome Jaquan, Sasha, it's all good here." Pook smiles and extends his hand to him. They eye them in suspense as he hesitates before taking it and they give an awkward half pound, half shaking hands. Pook does notice a burn scar on his wrist.

"Okay let's quit with the mushy stuff and get to this game and the drink! Lions are on damn it! They on a comeback! We missing it!" Tyrone huff's and flips on the big screen television.

"Comeback huh, that'll be the day." Jaquan snickers. They all look at him sideways before nodding in agreement. They all laugh and grab the appetizers and beer. Moe swipes chicken right out of a startled Zach's hand.

Detroit actually makes a good play as they yell and raise their drinks, "To Mama!"

Eat@Zeke's
Part IV:
Fine Like Wine

Cozy Wine

1 (750 milliliter) bottle red wine (such as Cabernet Sauvignon, Zinfandel, or Merlot)
1 orange, peeled and sliced
2/3 cup honey
1/4 cup brandy
3 cinnamon sticks
8 whole cloves, or more to taste
1 teaspoon grated fresh ginger

Combine red wine, orange slices, honey, brandy, cinnamon sticks, cloves, and ginger in a slow cooker.

Cook on Low until wine is steaming, 20 to 25 minutes.

Hyde Park, Chicago

Dreary black clouds roll across the windy-city skyline as the gusts the city is famous for blow hard against an upscale South-side loft. Rain splatters on the window pane beating the window senseless as if it is about to break. A neglected open window permits drops of water pooling on the hardwood floor. The antique wallpaper slowly peeling up. Against the odds its pane defiantly fights the oncoming torrent, slapping in a steady rhythm disregard by its occupants.

The darkened den is eerily quiet sans Mother Nature's beat-down outside as a stately grandfather clock chimes twelve midnight. A vibrating rumble joins the chorus as a cell phone hums diligently as it heads towards the edge of an office table. The ignored cell phone flashes twenty-seven missed calls before it rings once more, catapulting it over the edge. As it bounces, the cover and battery spring of. It comes to rest against a woman's foot covered up in the dark.

A house phone comes to life-disrupting the quiet complacency. The ignored answering machine picks up. A cheery message, excited female voices answer, "Hey, this is Maureen! And this is Bailey! You found us, now share with us! Toodles!"

A lit cigarette seemingly floats in mid-air as the silhouetted figure remains rigid in the dark, inhale, exhale, repeat, as toxic clouds escape out the window into the wet night. Silvia Wood's soft voice penetrates the room, "Maureen, sissy, please please answer the phone. I, I need my big sis please, I've been calling all day! Where are you? Are you there ignoring us? Please pick up!" She pauses for a moment before sighing softly, "Ezekiel is here, he flew back in today. Don't worry about him, you can do this Moe', he can't hurt you anymore, I have your back sis. I still can't find Kevin, the family is calling in from all over. I really, really don't know how long Mama has sis, this may be the last... I, I, I can't... I feel this is all my fault. Please call me, I can't do this anymore." Silvia's voice trembles and breaks up as she fades away before the final beep.

Soft sobs join the noisy spatter of rain outside as Maureen Wood's shaking hand picks up a glass of Versailles wine trying to drink. She sips the drink before attempting to light another cigarette, the glow from the lighter illuminates a picture of her and Mama in younger days. Mama Woods holds Little Moe in a happy shot amidst the home garden.

Maureen drifts off to those simpler times, reminiscing of running through the large garden playing as her mother busily plants zucchini, squash, corn, beets, radishes, greens, tomatoes and other plants that would end up in tasty dishes at Zeke's. Mama was cooking healthy organic goodies before it was the 'in' thing to do. Little Moe' would get under her mother's skirt, playfully chuck sprouts around before she got in trouble. Eventually, she wanted to help till the dirt and plant seeds herself. Mama and she shared a bond over gardening, spending hazy summer days in Detroit weeding and watering plants before sitting on a blanket in their yard sipping sweet tea enjoying the fruits of their labour.

"Mommy, does this plant grow pills?"

Mama would look around, concerned she had found something she shouldn't have before chuckling, "No baby, that's a green sprout, you're looking at the seeds!"

"Didn't you give this to me when my tummy hurt?"

"That was medicine made from man, I feed you green beans at dinnertime to nourish your soul."

"Oh, do I like these?"

"I sincerely hope so, they will help you grow big and healthy like your mother."

"Big and healthy? Oh no! I want to grow up to be as beautiful as you mommy."

Pausing, Mama about cries as she gives her daughter a tight hug, "You will dear, you will..."

It was a huge compliment. Everybody always said Little Moe was the spitting image of her mother. They felt her craft in the garden would lead her to fill Mama's shoes one day. But Little Moe always had loftier aspirations. She always looked forward to when Mama and Daddy Zeke would sell the excess food that didn't make it into the restaurant. With her caramel complexion, she would look stunning in her favorite yellow dress and act properly as a young businesswoman marketing their wares in the neighborhood. She would cut and paste pictures and put them on flyers to pass out, Mama would pay for small ads in the newspaper and she even perfected email blasts in the early days of the Internet.

Afterward, Daddy Zeke and Mama would take the family to the homeless shelter to personally give away all the unused produce and product. Maureen was extremely proud of that and her accomplishments under her mother's guidance. It helped make her into the gifted advertising executive she is today on Chicago's Michigan Ave. Always with a heart of gold, Moe lent a hand in community center and shelters when she could. It helped her meet Bailey, ironically a cook at one of the north-side's finest Italian eateries. Funny, even with all her accomplishments, her older brother's evil sass could destroy all her good vibes in one setting.

Ezekiel crossing her mind disrupts her happy thoughts like a skipped record, reminding her of the trouble Mama was in. Maureen emerges from her dark hiding spot, her dry makeup face blotched with dried tears. Her usual magnificently styled hair is dishevelled, her violet nightgown crumpled. Her near silent sniffles suddenly turn into loud sobs, her hands shaking. Her petite frame seems larger as she pushes the pictures off the display. Screaming, she grabs her wine glass and lobs it across the room, smashing it. She violently pushes everything off the desk before she breaks down crying uncontrollably.

The hallway light comes on as Bailey calls out, "Maureen baby? What's wrong? What's happening?" Maureen keeps weeping as Bailey is heard coming down the hallway. "Maureen? Where are you? Please talk to me!"

"Go back to bed, please Bailey!"

"No, I'm not Maurie, are you in the den?"

Bailey rounds the corner of the small office, flicking on the light to Maureen's disgust, her eyes squinting, "Damn It, turn out the flipping light!"

The equally petite Caucasian brunette adheres to her lovers' request. She rushes over to her, "Oh, my gosh, Maurie, what is wrong? Oh my gosh!"

Maureen holds her hand up, trying to keep the cook at bay but Bailey has a way of slipping past her defences every time. Years of mixing dishes have built her biceps up as she glides a tattooed arm around Maureen's, "Baby please talk to me, what happened? Please, please..."

Bailey caresses Maureen's face and manages to pivot her around to look into her eyes. Her eyes plead with Maureen who finally submits, "It's my Mama, I can't go on without her..." tears start to flow as she falls onto Bailey's bosom sobbing.

Bailey rocks her softly, comforting her lover by stroking her hair, "Shh, shh, its okay, I understand, I'm here for you Maurie, I'm always here for you. Let's pray for Mama..."

Thunder cracks in the distance as the immediate storm tapers off. The windowpane creaks a low squeaky groan in the dissipating breeze while the unwelcome gush of water inside retreats. The disarranged room falls back to its previous quietness as the darkness engulfs both ladies with Bailey rocking the love of her life to a more restful slumber.

West Bloomfield, MI (*Simmering)*

Harsh winds stir around a richly manicured garden estate leading up to a stately manor, seven bedrooms, large entrance-way, three baths, large living room to throw parties in, a kitchen large enough to have cooking shows, five car garage, swimming pool, guest house near a community lake, but it's all eerily empty, desolate. Oddly, it's still adorned with decorations from a child's previous birthday party, many of the party favors whipping about in the wind, unsealed trash bags toppled over with birthday wrap falling out. Lavish, but unkempt, the manor has been neglected for an obviously lengthy period.

A lone occupant mumbles incoherently amiss the howling wind as leaves and trash splatter against the grand windows on the upper deck. Kayla stirs in her sleep, sweating, kicks the covers off her as she groans, "Dirty backstabber..." Her nightmare assaults her fragile mind.

Detroit *(Boiling)*

Near the huge 'Made in Detroit' banner, a quiet brick laden office building business houses Simon Woods Simon. As office workers pore over clients' paperwork, lawyers rush back and forth to meetings and court dates. A large office in the back, clean, orderly, is uncommonly quiet as the receptionist desk sits empty. The network phone continuously blinks an ignored incoming call.

Kayla leans against her fire hot Tesla Roadster, dressed glamorously, yet offset by tears streaming, contorting her fabulously made-up face. Oblivious to passer-by's ogling her done up hair, sparkling gold earrings and necklaces draped down her ample bust in her crisp botanical Jason Wu dress, she obsesses instead her nicely manicured nails clutched around her iPhone constantly pressing redial.

Kayla grits her lipstick smudged teeth together, "Answer the damn phone..."

Annoyed with the business voicemail, Kayla switches her tactic, dials another number.

West Bloomfield *(Simmering)*

Kayla whimpers and shoots up out of bed. She looks around puzzled, the room blurry, not knowing where she is for a moment. Her hair frayed and unkempt, her robe dingy, no makeup, she looks as if she hasn't bathed in days. The wind bangs trash against the window as she jumps. Unconcerned, she scratches herself and eyes three thirty-four on the clock.

"This that bull..."

She opens her drawers and searches for something. Snorting, she looks around frantically before eyeing something on the floor, reaches, it's a small blue pill.

"What the doctor ordered!"

She grins and lays it on the nightstand, crushes it immediately with a handy metal device before proceeding to snort it. She kneels still for a moment as it drips down her cavity, letting it kick in before her eyes flutter and she blacks out kneeling against the nightstand. Her mind drifts off again...

Detroit *(Boiling)*

Inside Simon Woods Simon, Ezekiel leans back in his chair behind a large modern desk, acting as if studying the ceiling, his suit rumpled as if he has been working hard all day. A unique ringtone disrupts his thoughts as he looks forward. His Blackberry business cell phone lists 32 missed calls, but it's not what is ringing. He reaches into a hidden pocket of his sports suit and pulls out a small flip phone. He looks at the phone quite puzzled.

"Why are you calling me??"

Out of sight, Ms. Kane mumbles, "Obviously I'm not, just a little bit preoccupied..."

He answers, "Who is this?"

"It's your wife you egotistical moron. Think I wouldn't discover your secret phone? Do you take me for an idiot?!"

"Kayla? I..."

"Oh, now you know my name? Now you want to address me? Really? After I pleaded for you to acknowledge me for months? Years? Who do you think you are?"

"Now listen here..."

"NO! You listen to you son-of-a-bitch! No respect to your Mama; who's a great lady but her first seed sprouted fell far from the tree, rotten and awful, stinky like manure, just ripe for bottom-feeders, nasty parasites to discover and devour, fight over, destroy a happy-home, destroy a family! Those bottom feeding sluts can have my discarded left-overs! You deserve each other!"

"Baby, you're delusional, what are you talking about?! Nothing is going on!"

"Oh yeah, really? Delusional huh? I have your delusional!"

"Kayla, really, I'm trying to work here..."

She clicks the phone off on him.

West Bloomfield *(Simmering)*

Kayla's head nods, she hits the nightstand waking her up abruptly.

"Ouch! Dammit! Now I need another..."

Kayla achingly gets upright and starts to stumble about the room, searching, looking around for more of her beloved blue pills. She doesn't even notice the dark blood dripping from her forehead.

Barefoot, she meanders out into the hallway, leaning against the wall, her nose dripping. The extensive hallway sways like an extended tunnel. She whimpers, "Stop moving, and stay straight."

She manages her way to the stairs, looks down them, contemplating, stoic, nerved. Finally, slowly, she descends downwards, mumbling, "I don't remember living in a tower."

Halfway down, she slips on something and tumbles the rest of the way down. Flopping over herself she hits the bottom floor with a loud thud. Sprawled out on her stomach, she groans in pain, "Dammit, I'm firing that lackadaisical maid in the morning..." She pauses, remembers, "Oh wait, I already did!" Kayla starts to giggle manically over her own irony before she spots her blue friends on the living room coffee table. Her mouth contorts into a grim grin.

Detroit *(Boiling Point)*

Kayla paces in the gleaming sun glaring at the offices of Simon Woods Simon. "Work huh, you working hard huh, gotta bring home the bacon to your wife and kids huh?" She eyeballs her Tesla, "I have something that will work for you!"

Kayla pushes an unsuspecting pedestrian out of her way, "Move! Get out my way!" before entering her vehicle. They respond with a visual obscenity.

Ignoring them, she guns her electric sports car, turning up loud Detroit legend Adubb Da Gawd, rapping "Don't Shoot (Me Tonight)" Working the shift buttons she puts it in gear before darting out among surprised drivers. Vehicles swerve out of her way as she does an abrupt U-Turn in the middle of downtown. People honk and shout at her as she revs the engine louder, her tires burns rubber before darting across the street.

"Yay baby! Look at me go!"

She drops the throttle and races the Tesla across the street as cars dart out of the way. She bounces over the curb while startled pedestrians leap and roll out of the way. Splicing a newsstand in half, paper flies everywhere as the car bounces towards the plate glass bay windows of Simon Woods Simon. A loud sickening crash erupts as the car enters the building. Surprised office workers run for safety as office furniture and supplies fly into the air.

The Tesla bashes through the windows of Ezekiel Woods office raining glass down onto the floor. Kayla emerges from the bashed car, peeking over the dash. Quiet now except for broken lights flickering, something moves across the destroyed room. Her husband and Ms. Kane peek out from behind the desk.

"I got your delusional! Working so hard for your bloody money!" Kayla raises her iPhone and starts snapping shots.

Ms. Kane shrieks and grabs her top before fleeing to the restroom with Kayla snapping sequential shots. "Run slut! Run!"

Marty and Theodore Simon rush up with other office workers. "Great Googly! What in God's name is happening here!?" Theodore bellows as Marty looks in shock.

"Hi Marty! Hi Theo! Tell Clara I probably won't be making her bridal party this weekend but good luck with the nuptials! If you're a snake, like my beloved husband, she's gonna need it! Oh, and make sure to sue me well, because my money is his money, and he's part of you suckers! So, go at it ya-bitch!" Kayla shoots multiple pictures of their shocked faces.

Marty bellows, "I've always had respect for you Kayla, but this is clearly unacceptable!"

"Really? Really, office party so-called elevator mishap with the bellboy Marty... The BELLBOY Marty! What do you think Clara would think of that predicament? Hmmm?"

"Well, I what...I never!?" Several office workers snicker.

"Hmm-hmmm, sorry for the abrupt disclosure. Blame all this on your beloved partner, my so-called HARD-WORKING hubby!"

Ezekiel attempts to interrupt, "Kayla I..."

"Ahhh!! SHUT IT! This my moment, Zekey Jr. And now in the words of your beloved sis, 'Toodles! Ya Beech!'" Kayla tries to turn over the engine as the battered car stalls.

“I’ve had enough of this fiasco, someone get me the police on the phone now! This is unacceptable!” Theodore bellows.

"I hope there's no fire!" Marty quips. Theodore narrows his eyes at him.

The car turns over as loud hip-hop music disrupts the awkward scene, she backs up over office equipment as some associates attempt to race after her. She throws it into gear as the dislodged bumper rests on the floor tripping the close following workers. Kayla makes her escape back out the hole she made while onlookers look on in shock.

The partners glare at the beleaguered Ezekiel with contempt, who all he could do is shrug in contempt.

West Bloomfield *(simmered out)*

Utopia pulls up to the Woods manor in her Fiat, bobbing her head to Juny D's 'Hold On'. She shakes her head, “Mmmm, that boy is cute!"

Filing out of the car are Ezekiel and Kayla's eleven-year-old daughter Kylie and seven-year-old son Matador. Matador tumbles out of the car with Utopia's five-year-old son Milo. The boys spend so much time playing together they regard each other as brothers.

"Boy, come back here! Gimmie my ball!" Milo cries out as Matador sprints towards the garden.

"Come catch me!" Matador yells out now yards away.

"Boys! Mind the yard, I don't think Mr. Wright has been here for a while!" Utopia calls out.

Kylie yaks away on her iPhone, "Well no, I don't think Rafael is cute, that's you, I have higher standards. What? No, Kirk and I are just friends! I mean, he did try to kiss me once, but who told you that?"

Utopia eyes her in shock and scrunches her face, "Oh no, trying to do what I did..." She trails off as she is surprised by the locked door. She tries it again before ringing the doorbell. Nothing. She knocks hard as the tween annoys her talking like a grown woman.

Utopia looks through the small window to the left, "Maybe Isabella is not working either? The place looks horrible. Where is your mother? She knows we need to be at the hospital!"

Milo giggles, "Look at the funny car." The boys touch Kayla's smashed Tesla parked by the garage. Utopia gasps.

She looks through the small window to the right, knocking harder, she does a double-take eyeing something odd on the floor. She places her hand on her mouth, grabs Kylie who sees the same thing, Kylie drops her phone and screams.

"MOMMY!!"

Inside, Kayla lies sprawled out, lifeless on the floor, blue powder around her nose and mouth, an empty bottle of JW's fine wine, and vomit on the floor.

Eat@Zeke's
Pt. V:
Styles upon Styles

My life in the sunshine, everybody loves the sunshine,

Folks get down in the sunshine, folks get brown in the sunshine.

Just bees and things and flowers.

Feel what I feel, feel what I'm feeling in the sunshine.

Do what I do, do what I'm doing in the sunshine.

~Roy Ayers

Detroit

Poetic vibes ooze through Freddy Styles earbuds as he rounds another bend jogging on **Belle Isle** predawn early morning Detroit. A light drizzle sprinkles his face as suddenly the fog lifts and rays of sunshine peek through over the horizon, bounding across the waves of Lake Michigan from the Canadian border. Freddy takes a moment to soak in the majestic sunrise. He continues his fitness quest.

Back in the city, Freddy keeps pace through the streets. The 73-year-old is in better shape than many of the younger people he passes by. He bounces up the concrete stairs to the walkway above I-75 and crosses to the other side.

"Freddy! Que Pasa mane!" Jose, a local vendor setting up his clothing cart is familiar with Freddy's route. Freddy waves and keeps stepping.

"Yo Freddy my mans! You ready to get that platinum necklace for your lady ol' G?" Another vendor setting up holler's out.

"I hear ya, Stephen! Maybe next week when you find something not sprayed on!"

"Ah, why you call me out like that homie!"

"Maybe when you show me your official vendors license!"

Stephen waves his arms in defeat as Freddy disappears into the adjoining neighborhood.

Making his way back into his east side borough, Freddy keeps an eye out for problems. Being a member of the neighborhood watch, he takes it seriously when vandals want to destroy the remaining structures standing. With so many foreclosures and abandonment of neighborhood homes, it's just a shell of its former glory. Homeless, squatters, drug dealers, prostitutes, and other vagrants take up shelter causing more issues, or many are lost to thieves and arsonists scrounging for anything worth value.

Is a bittersweet irony that the once glorious Motor City succumbed to bankruptcy much as the automakers before them that built it.

Freddy has long been considered the rock of his neighborhood, running the community center, coaching baseball, a deacon at the church, an astute businessman. His immediate tight-knit neighbors reflect this as he rounds the corner from several burnt-out homes to a tree laced, clean, kept up paradise. Most of the homes on his block are still occupied, hold a decent value and everybody looks out for each other.

He breathes a sigh of relief, no new 'for sale' signs. It was unusually quiet this morning, even for it still being early.

His instincts kicked in, something was amiss. He was almost at his house when something out of the corner of his eye caught his attention. His across the street neighbor Gladys Wright was away for the week visiting relatives in St. Louis, so why was her kitchen window ajar?

Freddy flicks off the music and snaps a shot of the window. He steps forward to inspect further, his finger ready to call his detective contact Enrique Gonzales on speed dial. He hears something crash in her basement, he dials.

"Gonzales."

"It's Freddy, have some trespassers over at Ms. Wrights, I'm standing watch outside."

"Freddy, I'll have somebody on their way, now you just stand watchman, don't get in the way of police business!"

"Enrique, would I do that?"

He snickers, "Um, we're talking about Mr. Freddy Styles here, just stay down brother, we're on the way."

"Copy that." He hangs up the phone and moves towards the window as he hears chattering.

Two masked men emerge out of the window carrying bags of electronics and jewelry. The first one stumbles and catches his footing. The other struggles to get out with the heavy sack.

"Hey man, catch this."

"Hold on fool, I almost fell yo."

"Don't ruin that stuff negro, we bout to get paid!"

Freddy is recording the entire conversation; the first man suddenly notices him as the second finally gets out.

"You two aren't gonna get paid anything in prison!"

"The hell? Where'd you come from ol' man?" The second one glares at him as the other sprints.

"Yo let's roll!" The second one starts after him, "I'm not getting caught fo'sho!"

Freddy frowns, "Jaquan? Jaquan Mendelson? That you? Boy, what the Sam Hill?"

They stop in their tracks frozen before sprinting forward and jumping the fence, the second gasps, "What? How'd the old man make you fool?"

Jaquan shakes his head, continues up the fence.

"Boy, I know your mama! Your dad died in prison, do you want to follow in his footsteps? Boy, don't repeat his tragic mistake. I'm going to have to call your mama."

Jaquan pauses, "Wait, don't do that."

"Crap fool, I'mma have to take out this ol' man! What the hell!" The second thug pulls out a switchblade. He steps towards Freddy who doesn't flinch.

Sirens are heard in the distance as Jaquan starts to panic, "Did you already call the cops?!"

Freddy nods as he looks for her number, "Oh yes boy, and I'm looking for your mother's number."

"Damn yo! I'mma bust grandpa's head wide open!" The boy lunges at Freddy, he blocks the attack and grabs and twists the boys' arms behind his back before putting him into a choke-hold. The boy is in shock, squirming.

"Dang it young man, made me mess up my search."

"Freddy, hey man, don't call my mama, she gone yo."

The boy struggling in the hold gasps as he looks at them both.

"What you mean gone?"

Jaquan pulls off his mask, sighs as he licks his lips.

"Boy, I asked you a question, what you mean she's gone?"

The boy keeps struggling with Freddy's hold. "The hell?! Why you two just chatting? J, bust this ol' man! I don't give a f..."

Freddy quickly squeezes the boy neck in a chokehold, knocking him out, "Oh shut it, young man, talk too much!"

"Did you kill him?"

"Naw, he just sleep. He'll be alright. Do you want to be alright?"

Jaquan shrugs, not sure what to say as the sirens come closer.

"Boy, do you want to chat with my friends coming or talk to me?"

"Man, what we gonna talk bout man?"

"A better future for you. Can be a moron with your buddy here or maybe let me help guide you on a better plan."

"All right man, don't be no funny stuff. I'll see what you talkin' bout fo'sho."

"Cool then, come on hurry up."

Freddy drops the bags and knife on the boy's chest as he rolls over and snores. They quickly walk across the street to Freddy's house as cop cars come flying around the corner.

Freddy opens the door as Jaquan hesitates, "Son, I'm not a crazy serial killer, get your fool butt in there so we can figure this out."

They go inside as the police arrive. They spot the snoring boy holding the bags and surround him.

They watch the arrest as other curious neighbors arrive to spectate. Police lift the handcuffed boy to the cruiser. They take off his mask as he looks around bewildered, drool on his lips.

"Hey, where am I? I was on my way to get ice cream."

"Yeah right kid, in the car you go."

"Wait, I want to order pistachio." The boy murmurs as they hold his head into the vehicle.

Enrique arrives, notices the boys confusion, "What's wrong with him?"

The arresting officer shrugs, "I don't know, it's how we found him."

Enrique looks over at Freddy's house, shakes his head, but then smiles and nods. Freddy nods back in his bay window.

"I want ice cream!" The boy yells in the cruiser.

Freddy shakes his head and walks away from the window, "So sit down boy, what's this mess about your mama? I know I haven't seen her in church for good over a month or two."

"She gone sir." Jaquan sinks into the seat.

"Gone? She on a trip? She pass away? I can't help you I don't know what you're talking about. Lay it out kid."

Jaquan acts out cooking and ingesting crack cocaine. Freddy huffs and sits down in shock, "She used to be doing so well, she was what, the auto financier down at Mel's Auto Sales? Was at church every week, what happened?"

Jaquan sighs, looks out the window, "Life."

They sit in silence for a moment, watching the cops investigate across the street.

"You want a soda boy?" Jaquan nods yes as Freddy goes to his refrigerator. He brings back a cola and orange juice.

"Thanks."

"Really sad to hear about your mother. Isn't there a younger child at the house?"

Jaquan nods, "My little brother, Jory." He casually turns music on his phone, Flatbush Zombies "Friday."

Freddy wipes his face, looks at Jaquan bewildered before banging his juice on the table, "Turn that crap off boy! What the hell are you gonna do? Thievery isn't the answer, you're not a moron, you know better. What, go sell some poison on the streets? Same poison killing your moms? This Detroit kid, they gonna eat your young ass alive and you gonna end up in prison, just like your pops! Or worse, in an unmarked grave. Is that what you want? Or you gonna do something about it?"

Jaquan looks perplexed, "I dunno man, I dunno."

"Is that your final answer? Really? Boy, you have your diploma, a G.E.D? Something?"

"No, nothing man, I dropped out in the eleventh grade."

"You just ready to be another statistic kiddo, shame, shame. And what's going to happen to Jory in all this mess? Big brother is setting a perfect example for him by being a hot mess. Good job kid, his fate rests on your shoulders you dig what I'm saying?"

Jaquan sighs and shuffles in his seat as he takes another drink.

"Boy are you listening?!" Freddy stands up practically lurching at him. Jaquan spills the soda.

"Yeah man, yes sir, yes!" Jaquan looks at him in amazement.

"Boy, a job would be your first step. Gotta step up and be a man."

Freddy makes a call, Pook answers, "Zeke's Kitchen, come eat at Zeke's and get a half off coupon for your next visit."

"Pook, don't you guys need a dishwasher?"

"Freddy! What's up man? Um, yeah, we lost one in all the chaos with Mama."

"I have a young man ready to come down and wash." Jaquan looks at him puzzled.

"What? Half these kids hate washing dishes, they run for the hills. Who you got man? They going to stay?"

"Oh yes, he's going to stay, if he knows what's good for him. I have Jaquan Mendelson ready to go, when you need him?"

"Jaquan? That the same kid who, what the heck, Freddy man, he done tried to rob the store..."

"And Mama bailed him out and offered him the job then, Pook, trust, she'll okay this, and the kids will be okay, I need you to okay this now. I ever do you wrong man?

"Well I, no, but..."

"But nothing Pooky, when you need him, he ready."

Pook groans as he realizes this is a no-win battle, "Ugh, okay tell the boy he can come by four pm. He better be on time, I'm going to be watching him!"

"Four pm tonight, done deal, he'll be there!"

Freddy clicks off the phone, glares at Jaquan downshifting in his seat. "Okay, I don't suggest just anybody, this my name on the line. I need you to show me your skills."

"Do what?"

Freddy gets up and runs the hot water in his sink, pours the soap. Jaquan watches. Freddy looks at him, "Boy, the sink is not going to bite you, get your butt over here!"

Jaquan jumps up, "Yes sir, I didn't understand."

"Boy, you have a lot to learn. I'm sorry son that you're in this situation, it's not entirely your fault, but you have a lot of responsibility thrust on your shoulders right now. I'll talk to the ladies at the church and see if we could set up some type of intervention for your mother. You should be concentrating on education and your future. Right now, lil' bro needs you. So, you need to wash a dish."

Freddy holds the dirty plate to Jaquan who stares at it before finally accepting. He washes, shows it to Freddy. "Missed a spot son, let's do it again." They continue until he gets it right.

"Slayed are those who fell victim to the pipe,

A drug-controlled substance contained in a vial,

Set up by the devil as he looks, and he smiles,

Good at the game of tricknology,

But I have knowledge of myself, you're not fooling me."

~Grand Puba

Evening;

Freddy sits in front of Mama's bed, dressed in a brown corduroy suit, he places a white rose on her chest.

"Ms. Tyla Monroe, girl I remember when you first showed up off that Greyhound from Ohio. OMG, was the prettiest little thing I'd ever seen, I about passed out. Those lips were to die for. I thought I had me a nice new lil' girlfriend. And then my dear friend Ezekiel Sr. stepped up and stole your heart. You two were inseparable ever since and I was none the happier for my good friends. We've all been through a lot, the marches and the riots, the weddings, the births, the funerals, this last decade it's been worse than ever around here, but your love of life has persevered. It's been a wild ride Ms. Tyla. Life wouldn't have been the same over the last fifty years without you, definitely wouldn't have been none the better."

Freddy reaches and holds her hand for a moment, her thumb twitches, touches him back. Freddy smiles.

He continues, "Why I remember that one time when those skunks showed up behind the restaurant and you scooped them up before they could do anything..."

"Life can be only what you make it,

When you're feeling down you should never fake it,

Say what's on your mind and you'll find in time,

That all of the negative energy will all decrease."

~Mary J. Blige

Eat@Zeke's Part VI: Agape Soufflé

Sweet Potato Soufflé

3 cups mashed sweet potatoes
3/4 cup white sugar
1/3 cup butter, softened
2 eggs
1 teaspoon vanilla extract
1/2 cup milk
1 cup flaked coconut
1/3 cup all-purpose flour
1 cup packed brown sugar
1 cup chopped walnuts (or pecans)
1/3 cup melted butter

Preheat oven to 350 degrees F (175 degrees C). Combine the mashed sweet potatoes with the white sugar, soft butter or margarine, beaten eggs, vanilla and milk. Spoon into a 2 quart ovenproof baking dish.

Combine the coconut, flour, brown sugar, chopped nuts and melted butter. Sprinkle over the top of the sweet potatoes. Bake at 350 degrees F (175 degrees C) for 30 to 35 minutes.

Detroit

Un-noticed by two-legged passer-by, A fat orange Tabby cat stalks through tall grass. His focus is square on a red-breasted Robin, waddling obliviously in the small pool of water. Not even the black squirrel busy looking for food disturbs him. The Tabby ducks, his twitching tail the only part of his body noticeable. His location is unfortunately comprised by an annoying rat terrier who suddenly appears yapping insanely. The horrible lil' thing is cloaked in some type of thick looking bright two-legger material as he leads his human past the small yard.

Flustered, he takes his one opportunity to launch his attack as the spooked bird slips away unharmed. Something fuzzy bobs on the nearby fence as a female two-legger comes close, leaves something before walking away. Determined, the Tabby waits for her to leave before sprinting and bouncing at the swaying fuzz. He sinks his fangs into his prey. Suddenly a black shadow envelope him, hissing, shrieking and yowling. The Tabby's mouth is agape, hissing, but the black cat protecting his turf battles vigilantly freaking the orange feline away.

"Oh snap! Where those dang pesky cats come from?!" A woman leaving a teddy bear by the fence sprints away to the confines of her vehicle

The black cat proudly twitches his tail reclaiming his territory. This yard, this home is his and they better recognize. He lets out a satisfied yowl before continuing his rounds.

Oddly, his human, the older one, has been absent the last few days. He misses her dearly, she feeds him and takes care of him properly. The younger one, while kind to him is a bit more haphazard with his care. He walks the crest of his beloved fence to survey his neighborhood daily, ensuring everything is okay. Strangely, it recently keeps getting decorated by the passing two-leggers, leaving trinkets, cards, dolls, stuffed animals, candles, pictures, and strange food replicas. Most of this tribute to Mama Woods meant nothing to the protective cat besides being fodder to play with, such as the fuzzy top that lured in the Tabby.

"Oh, my goodness, Nightmare! Is that you? Oh, my!" The voice was shockingly familiar! Could it be? The cat became excited.

The female was exiting a taxi cab with quite a few carry along bags, big funny glasses that made her look like a bug, her hair done in rows. She is wearing a fluffy faux fur coat in spring weather that looked like it could have been one of the cat's relatives, feathery leggings, and spiked leather heels high enough to kill somebody.

"Nightmare, you silly rascal! How I missed you so!" Not worried, Nightmare lets gloved hands scoop him up. He smelt her familiar scent, how it had been so long. Oh goodness, Nightmare was excited, he hadn't seen his beloved MoMo, his original human in several cat lifetimes! He nuzzles up to her as she strokes his silky jet-black hair, taking the intimidating walk up to her childhood home, mouth agape.

Mama's quaint little home still was the showcase of the block with its orangish yellow siding, sky blue trim, huge wrap around porch that held many family and neighborhood bar-b-ques. Her yard, still fully lush with vegetation, flowers and a small fragment of her vegetable garden of yore.

Rattling the front door to no answer Maureen peers through the screen door, "Silvia baby? Baby girl I'm here!"

The only answer she hears is the faint sound of loud music somewhere towards the back of the home. She knocks again to her dismay as Nightmare attempts to tap the door with his paw mimicking her. The door not giving in, she walks around the long porch peering in windows. "Silvia girl! Your big sis is here! Open up!"

Silvia finds the kitchen door open and pushes in, Nightmare spots his half-empty bowl and yowls. "Oh honey, have you been fed? Tsk, tsk." Maureen finds his food and fills it up and changes his water. "Lil' sis needs to show and prove, or I may have to cart you back to the Chi to live with me and Bailey." She ponders on the reality of the situation. She walks over to a wall of pictures, she traces her long fingernail over pictures of her mother and father. She sighs, wipes a tear away before seeing a picture of Ezekiel and his wife, makes sure to put it on its face.

She hears a rumble and odd noises coming from the den. She walks towards it as the muffled music gets louder, "Toodles Silvia baby, is that you? What are you doing?"

The den's sliding doors are shut tightly, she fumbles with them, "I didn't even know these worked!"

She finally manages to pop the doors open as they bang to the side. Maureen is greeted with Silvia screaming, "OH MY! Shut the door! Shut the door!"

Maureen's eyes go wide, "Great googles! What the world!?"

Silvia screams again, throws a shoe to Nightmare's surprise as he runs off hissing, "Shut it! Shut it!" Maureen submits and shuts them, clasps her open mouth in shock.

Silvia shuts off the loud music of JoJo singing "Take the Canyon", something crashes as you hear her rustling and fumbling in the room. She emerges several minutes later, disassembled, and flustered, her clothes and hair a mess. She stands in the doorway and looks over at her sister perched on a bench by the staircase, legs crossed, gloves and coat still on, she peers over her dark bug glasses. Silvia blushes and grins, "Um, hi sis! You're here!"

Maureen shakes her finger, "Don't um, hi sis me young lady! What the heck was you doing in there with that, that, device? Were you, um, chatting with somebody?"

Silvia blushes twenty shades of crimson, "Um yeah, my boyfriend."

"Boyfriend? Like that?! Where is this boy, Mama didn't say anything about you having a man? Where is this fellow? Going to have a long talk with lover boy..."

"Um, Mama doesn't know about him. Please don't say anything."

"Do what? How you hide this critter? Where this boy hiding, I'll be that somebody to have a real chat with this..."

"He doesn't even live around here, he's not even in this state."

Maureen looks at her sideways, "Say what?" She shakes her head as she helps her sister adjust her clothes.

"You didn't even tell me you were coming! We can only chat by Skype, I thought I was alone!"

"Yeah, I see, what the boy in the armed forces or something? You meet at school?"

"No, no, um, he not even from here." Maureen looks at her dumbfounded. "Okay okay, I met him online, happy?"

Maureen's mouth drops again, "What, what, what?! Seriously?! Silvi! Heavens! This is some random boy online? Oh, Mama said you were stuck on Facebook and Twitter and IG! Holy crap! Have you ever even seen him besides pictures? Anybody else knows about this? I have to call..."

Silvia leaps for her sister, "No no no! Nobody knows, except you now! You can't, please sis, no. I love him."

Silvia pleads with her eyes as Maureen looks at her dumbfounded, "You're serious about this boy, aren't you? Love is a mighty strong word for somebody you've never met. You sure this isn't a catfish moment? Sis, I'm worried about you."

"No, no need to be worried, I can handle myself. I know he's real, I've talked to him on the phone, we've sent letters. Sis, I feel him, he's here." She touches her chest, looks longingly out the window.

"Oh boy..." Maureen sits back down shaking her head. "So, how far away is this boy, he's not across the continent is he? Somewhere overseas?"

"Um, no, he's down in Dayton."

"Really, in Ohio? That's close, it's near Mama's side of the family. A good what, three-hour drive? Time to make that road trip." Maureen picks Nightmare backup who was rubbing on her ankle, he purrs in her arms.

"Hey, what? A road trip? Now maybe that's not necessary..."

"Oh, now you don't want to meet this boy? This love of your life?"

"Um, well, I..."

"Okay, take me to see my mother then we making that move!"

"Seriously?"

"Seriously, you ready to meet this man, if he even is a man, or you scared?"

Silvia swallows hard, "Um..."

"Then it's settled! Road trip! Now baby sis, take me to see my mother!" Silvia stands dumbfounded, mouth agape as Mo finds her keys and grins, walks outside to her car, "Come sister! This car is not going to drive itself!"

Silvia groans and submits, she knew once her sister was committed to a cause, resistance was futile. Nothing but sisterly love here.

Detroit Hospital

Silvia pulls her Ford Focus into the hospitals parking garage when her sister, up to now calm cool and collected turns stark white. "Mo, what's wrong?"

Maureen gasps, clutches Silvia's hand tightly, she can barely speak, "You, you...

"What sis, what?"

She points, "You, you didn't say he was going to be here."

Silvia looks at the row of cars perplexed, "What? Who?"

"The demon incarnate, I'm not ready. We gotta go."

"The who what, sissy you're freaking me out."

"Woods Jr. I'm not ready."

Silvia finally realizes she's referring to Ezekiel's BMW sitting the next row up, Silvia sighs as their feud has been lasting far too long. She suggests, "It can't be him, he should be at work. It's probably Kayla using his car."

"No, no, my gut says it's him, OMG?" Maureen starts breathing hard.

"Sis, chill, I'll call his work."

"I need some air." Maureen gets out and paces back and forth as Silvia makes the call.

Silvia gets out of the car, "Come on sis, they said he's with his wife on important business, come on, they probably left his car and took hers."

Maureen bites her lip, "Ugh, I hope so. I'm not going to let him faze me to see Mama. Maureen be strong, Maureen be strong, breathe, have to remember my steps." Silvia looks at her skeptically as they enter the hospital.

"Do you want to get her a gift? We could go to the gift shop."

"Baby girl, I already have something, most importantly, I'm here. Any word from Kevin?"

"Nothing, we're still looking."

"Both of our brothers are douches." Maureen stops in her tracks, mouth agape.

"Mo? Now what?"

"Douche huh, good to see you too sis. Surprised you even came out of your closet to see your mother." Silvia turns face to face with Ezekiel glaring at Maureen.

"See what I mean sis! I knew we shouldn't have come! I'm not ready to see the devil incarnate! I can see mother later!"

"That's right dear sis, run like you usually do. Mother's been better off without you around anyways. Devil huh? Guess you don't remember what happened in the city of Sodom to the likes of you."

Maureen turns around and slaps Ezekiel to his surprise, "As if! It was destroyed for wicked people so look at yourself! I'm not letting you ruin my visit to see mother! Stay out of my way!"

Maureen pushes him out of the way as he holds his stinging face, Silvia smirks at him, "You so deserved that."

"Is no matter, let her have her short-lived victory. I have bigger problems currently, I'm here trying to find my wife. She never picked up the kids and hasn't been answering the phones. Have you talked to her?"

"Oh, my goodness, no."

"I heard she may be here. If you'll excuse me. You can take care of Jezebel." He turns to leave.

"Maureen, her room is this way." Silvia huffs.

"Oh, my goodness, Woods family, I'm so glad you're here! Come quickly!" Silvia turns to see Freddy Styles approaching quickly.

Ezekiel turns around also, "Fred, what's the matter, is it Mama?"

"Afraid so, she's awake, but she's not right!"

Ezekiel and Silvia look at each other before rushing off to the room.

Freddy takes a breath as Maureen slips up behind him, "Oh my goodness, Freddy Styles is that you?"

Freddy turns and gasps, mouth agape, "Oh my stars, look what the cat dragged out, it's not lil' Ms. Motown, Maureen Woods in the flesh!"

They embrace warmly, "Aw, always loved your big teddy bear hugs Freddy Styles, and you were always my favorite! I had such a crush on you when I was little."

Freddy holds her arms and gives her a puzzled look, "What, wait...?"

She giggles and playfully punches him in the arm, "Hey, I always recognized what a good soul you were, you're a legend in the neighborhood, and those fancy purple suits, OMG! Was so handsome! And still are!" He smiles slyly, not sure how to respond. "Trust, I was with a man once, you are the prototype!"

He blushes, "You always have such a way with words young lady. I do miss your bright sunshine around here. I think you better go and see your mother. I'll show you to the room."

Mama is being seen by Doctor Sharon checking her vitals, a nurse assists. Mama's eyes are half closed as she looks distraught.

Silvia and Ezekiel barge in, "Mama, mother, are you okay?"

Dr. Sharon glares at them, "I'm sorry, no visitors right now. Your mother is suffering a relapse, I need you to wait outside."

"Mama! Mama no!" Silvia pleads, tears up.

"Nurse, please escort the Woods to the reception room!"

"Doctor, we have a right to be here to see our mother. What are you doing to her?" Ezekiel bellows.

The doctor sighs, "I need to stabilize her blood pressure, she's 160 over 146 and that's not good. If you would give me a moment to..."

Mama grunts, "Kevin? Is that you?"

Ezekiel groans, "No Mama, its little Zeke."

"Mama?" Maureen holds a lily as she enters, the room grows quiet.

Mama turns to the voice, "My baby."

The heartbeat seems to stabilize as Maureen grasps Mama's hand, "Mama, I'm here." She places the lily in her weak hands. Mama tightens her grip around her hands.

"Baby..." She gasps, weak, her heart rate starts to rise.

"Please, let me get her stabilized." The doctor pleads.

"Wait, baby girl, find Ponyi Patel."

"What? Mama?" Maureen starts to tear up seeing her mother struggle.

"What is that, does she know what she's saying?" Ezekiel injects.

"What is that?" Silvia gasps, holding her hands together.

"Find Ponyi, you find...Kevin." Mama groans and passes out.

"Woods family! Please!" Dr. Sharon and the nurses work diligently on her. A nurse shuffles them out to the reception area.

"What is a Ponyi? That a game?" Silvia whines.

"I don't think she knew what she was talking about. This is incredible." Ezekiel shakes his head, pulls out his cell phone. Freddy gives Maureen a hug.

The nurse shakes her head, "Ponyi Patel is a woman, and she visited your mother a day ago. I can't say anything else but that may help." She disappears into the room leaving the Woods and Freddy's mouths agape. The family love was being challenged.

Eat@Zeke's
Part VII:
Gumbo Elixir

Creole Gumbo

4 bone-in chicken breast halves, with skin
8 chicken thighs
1 white onion, chopped
1 green bell pepper, chopped
1/2 cup all-purpose flour
1/2 cup butter
1-pound Creole smoked sausage
2 1/2 cups water
1-pound shrimp
2 tablespoons Cajun-style seasoning

Boil chicken breasts and thighs with onion and bell pepper in a large pot of salted water, for about 40 minutes or until cooked through and no longer pink inside. Drain, debone chicken and set aside.

In a large saucepan stir together flour and butter over low heat to make a roux; add boiled chicken, sausage and water and bring all to a boil. Cover saucepan and simmer over low heat for about 1 1/2 hours. Add shrimp and simmer for about 1 more hour, then add seasoning to taste and serve.

Arcadia

A heart monitor beeps softly in steady repetitive prose, a quiet harmony in the oddly desolate hospital hallway. The darkened hallway is lit with just emergency lights as the wind howls outside rattling the windows. A continuous squeak draws closer permeating the air obnoxiously.

Kayla emerges trudging slowly, long IV's attached to her arms as she lugs the machine behind. She looks horrible, bags under her eyes, bruises on her body, hair dishevelled, eyes glazed over as she looks around perplexed.

She purses her chapped lips together, barely whispers, "Hello?"

Nobody answers in the vacant ward as she continues her quest. She peers into patient rooms where they sleep peacefully, not to be disturbed.

She meekly asks, "Hello?" Still no response.

She finds a staff lounge and meanders through, it's vacant.

"Why isn't anybody here?"

She arrives at the opposite hallway directly in front of Mama's room. She peers in, she's gone.

"Looking for me?"

Kayla whips around almost dropping the machine, Mama stands upright, basking in the glow of the humming fluorescent light.

"Mama, you're okay." Tears stream down her face.

"I've been better, you don't look so hot yourself. Maybe you had the heart attack and I'm sitting up in that huge mansion."

"That mansion and Ezekiel is why I'm here. I hate to say it..."

"Don't make excuses for my son, but don't make excuses for yourself either."

"But Mama, you don't..."

"I don't want to hear it. What, you think I was born yesterday? I know my son can be a pain, I understand relationships have issues, I understand life is hard, welcome to the real world. So, you reckon teaching my grandbabies that coping out overdoing prescription drugs is the answer to life's problems?"

"I don't reckon anything..."

"You make your bed dear, you lay in it. People have been going through these same issues for years. You come to that fork in the road where you either fight to win, hold your head up keeping the faith. Or be a yellow baby and run and hide behind your manufactured pills the man served you nice and cold. Numb yourself to reality."

"I don't do anything illegal, I stick with my scripts..."

"And they say the Devil works in mysterious ways, sometimes he's quite obvious."

Mama squeezes her hand hard as she tries a faint smile.

Kayla sits up abruptly in her darkened hospital room, stares right into the eyes of her husband Ezekiel standing at the foot of her bed. He slightly leans forward, glaring back at her, the whites of his eyes illuminated in the dim night lighting. She stares back in silence; the only sound is of her heartbeat. Her lips start to quiver, she grips the sheets swallowing hard as the veins on her neck shows. Ezekiel narrows his eyes, stares at her predicament indifferent. Pee stain develops on her bed sheets as her eyes flutter and go back into her head as she shakes. The fluorescent lights blur as the room fades to black.

Ezekiel's voice looms in hard and cold repeating her name, "Kayla...Kayla!"

In the early morning, Kayla awakes in her bed disoriented, confused. Her mind playing tricks on her as the silhouette of Ezekiel burns on the empty wall. She pulls her arm and groans in pain with the IV tubes wedged deeply. She groans, sits up dishevelled, a hot mess, shaking, she writhes and screams until hospital staff comes to her aid.

In the nearby waiting room, Utopia grabs the boys hands, "Hey, want to go play some video games in the lounge? Let's go."

Matador and Milo take her hand eagerly, pulling on her, "Let's go! Come on!"

Kylie stays rooted in her seat, gripping her tablet, trembling, and dried tears on her face. Utopia sighs, bites her lip, "Kylie baby, you want to join us?"

Kylie sniffles, shakes her head, "I can't."

"I know this is hard sweetie, you want to talk..."

"Can I go ahead to school?"

"You sure you want..."

"Yes, I'm positive."

Utopia nods yes as she makes the call to arrange it. She puts her hand on Kylie's shoulder who turns burrowing her face into Utopia's chest hugging her tightly. Utopia tries not to tear up as the driver answers.

Downtown Detroit

"Listen, Marty, once the defendant realizes we have an ace in the hole in our presentation they will have no choice but to fold and crumble like cake. They are unravelling like cheap glue. Let's stay on course that we laid out before circumstances abruptly changed..." Ezekiel rattles on his cell phone in a busy Detroit downtown eatery. Miss Kane sits across from him picking away at a gourmet salad as she watches intently his hurried speech, his fixation of tapping his stir stick obnoxiously on his double mocha fudge slightly whipped coffee. Her thoughts wandering to better times with her boss and moderate lover, then reality hits.

Ezekiel checks his call waiting annoyed, "Hang on Marty, somebody is blowing up my line. Guess my voicemail wasn't good enough for them." He hits the button, "Hello, who is this?" His face goes from irreverent to concern.

"Excuse me, how did you get this number?"

"Isn't any matter how I got your number. You knows I'm not going anywhere, bout time for you to fess up and handle your business you've neglected for so long. No better time than the present to fulfil your destiny." The deep female voice booms over his cell irritating him to no end.

"Excuse me? Are you really threatening me? Do you not know who I am and what I'm capable of? I will crush you." Miss Kane arches her eyebrow surprised.

"I heard Mo is back."

"And? Really, you bore me, good day."

"Wait, it's bout time she knows the truth. Bout time everybody knows the truth. I've respected your parent's legacy so long. While Mr. High and Mighty plays the wicked games lawyers play; your real dirt has always been right below the surface. Trust and believe I have the proof to shut you down."

"Really now? Shut me down. And what fantasy proof is this? You make me laugh."

"And you make me laugh. Everybody knows what goes on in the dark always sees the light. Funny is you know how Detroit winters are always brutal, and coldness has a way of preserving discarded material thought gone forever."

Ezekiel's face goes white, his stir stick drops to the floor as Miss Kane almost chokes on her salad, never seeing him this caught off guard.

His voice booms louder, "Don't you dare it! That evidence would be clearly inadmissible and never fly in court! Witch you hear me!?" He bangs the tiny table much to the chagrin of nearby surprised patrons.

His face softens, "Oh wait, Marty? Oh heavens, my apologies, oh goodness, I..." He rubs the sweat off his brow clearly distraught. "It went through, the judge okayed the motion? Oh brilliant. Crap, hang on Marty!"

He flips calls again, "Now listen here, I will slap a lawsuit on you so fast..." His motions change again to bewilderment.

"Oh wait, who is this? Pook?" He frowns. "Do what? What is this concerning? Oh, you're at the restaurant, oh yes, the black chubby midget." He pauses. "Right. Listen, I'm quite busy right now, what is it? A health inspector? Not up to code? Interesting." His face changes to indifference as Miss Kane looks on amazed.

"Okay, okay, right, I see. And where is my sister, you didn't tell her this trivia? Is she hunting Indians? Excuse me?" He shakes his head antsy. "Listen, Pokey, do what my mother would have done or shut it down. It's no matter to me in this instance." He hangs up.

"Marty? Okay good, listen, that other situation? Might be resolving itself, stay tuned. Yes, I know, is ironic..."

Miss Kane pushes her food aside and gets up abruptly, exhausted of hearing his mess. He pauses for a moment to look in her direction as she leaves before a waitress delivers the bill.

A nearby patron's cell phone ringer buzzes loudly playing Big K.R.I.T.'s "Hydroplaning." Ezekiel wrinkles his nose, "Excuse me, sir, could you turn down your rap crap? Nobody wants to hear that mess."

The man frowns at him and smirks, "Why, it sounds too much like your theme song you bourgeois bastard? Get out of here!"

Ezekiel sucks his lips for once caught speechless, disarmed he goes about his business.

Zeke's Diner

"Listen, this is the second major violation in six months, I'm sorry the city of Detroit and the state of Michigan won't tolerate these instances. We're going to have to shut you down immediately before this causes an outbreak." A thin balding Health Inspector in a cheap suit is walking backward out of Zeke's Kitchen trying to avoid Pook and Tanya glaring angrily in his face.

Tanya taps at him, "You're full of it! You know that first 'so-called' violation turned out to be a mistake by the 'then' inspector and was dismissed! Mama keeps pristine care of this kitchen sucka!"

"And she's not present, is she? And that record still stands, section 4528, code..."

Pook hangs up the phone frustrated with Ezekiel's response, "Listen, dog, that's here nor there, we'll get that straightened out in court. Something with this doesn't feel right, give us some time to figure this out..."

Two Detroit police officers arrive by the counter as eating patrons take notice. Suga watches while cooking, glaring at the escalating tension, her nostrils flare as he keeps jabbering. She puts down her pot to watch what the health inspector is finding in the walk-in cooler.

Big Moe munching on chili with Zach grunts loudly, Zach asks, "Hey what's going on?"

The first officer eyes the patrons getting antsy, "Is none of your concern sir. It's almost closing time anyway."

Suga shakes the pan confiscated by the health inspector, removes his tagging.

Tanya is in his face, "You know you don't have no right, you need to get out of..."

He spots Suga behind her, "Ma'am, that's evidence, please put that down!"

The second officer calls in backup concerned about the escalating chaos as the first tries to scoot by Tanya and Pook arguing with the inspector, "Ma'am you heard the inspector!"

Moco watches concerned from the serving floor.

Suga turns her large frame around thwarting them as she sniffs the raw chicken.

"Ma'am you're interfering with an official investigation!" The inspector attempts to move past Pook who gets in his way.

"Hey, listen to me, I'm saying something ain't right here, Mama would never have left anything that would hurt her customers..."

"And I said she's not..."

"We follow her lead sir, you're not listening."

"Sucka, you need to step!" Tanya is in his face as outside another police cruiser arrives.

"What is going on? Pooky, Tanya, calm down!" Moco moves towards the counter as the additional officers arrive.

"They trying to shut down Zeke's!" Tanya says aloud. The patrons chattering turns into an uproar.

Suga backs the officer into shelving as she grunts and lifts a huge chicken thigh and leg up over her head, waving it back and forth.

"Ma'am you sealed the case! Shut this place down immediately!" The inspector yells.

"Wait, wait, she's trying to tell you something! Damn!" Pook cringes as the second officer pushes past him and Tanya towards Suga.

Moe is standing as the additional officers' move in, "Moe love Zeke's! Listen, they said mistake!"

The officers pull out their batons, "Sir, this is not your concern! Will ask you kindly to leave now!"

"Oh, hell no, you guys aren't shutting down Zeke's, no way there's a problem with their food!" Zach stands up also.

Jaquan washing dishes, peeks around the corner to see what's happening. The second officer spots him, "Hey! We've been looking for you!"

Jaquan's eyes blinks in shock as he drops a plate and sprints towards the back door, the second officer chases after him forgetting his first mission.

Suga pushes her way towards the health inspector gripping the dripping raw chicken. Pook shakes his head understanding her, "Hey, hey! Suga says this isn't even our meat! That is the mistake!"

"And? It's in your establishment! You want Zeke's to be responsible for a salmonella outbreak? It's covered in nasty bacteria you're serving your so-called family!"

"Damn, she's right, that's not even our meat! What the hell? Did you plant this? You setting us up because Mama isn't here?"

The health inspector purses his lips, scoffs as he shakes his head, "What? Excuse me? And what advantage would I have to..."

Suga grunts and waves the meat by his head as he ducks, the drippings splash him as he wipes himself furiously. The first officer grabs at her arms to no avail. Upset diners are keeping the joining officers at bay. More officers are called.

A patron yells. "They trying to close Zeke's!"

Another patron shouts out. "I'm calling my cousins, they can't do this!"

Moco is caught up in the swell as people start showing up out of nowhere, "Did anyone call Silvia or the family?"

More officers arrive, cherries and berries ablaze as the restaurant melee is getting out of hand. "Stand down, stand down! This doesn't have to get any worse! With so many violations you can't afford the lawsuits this escalating situation is going to cause. Do the right thing and shut this down right now!" The inspector is in Pook's face as his toupee shakes off his head. Pook shakes his head.

The police back off the crowd, pushing them out of the diner as they start to chant in unison, "Eat at Zeke's! Eat at Zeke's! Eat at Zeke's! Eat at Zeke's!

"No sucka, you don't get it, the neighborhood won't let that happen. As I said, we don't make mistakes, this so-called food has been planted here and we'll prove it! You can trust Zeke's food I guarantee it!" Pook is in the inspector's face.

"They trying to do us like Flint!" Tanya wails. A customer spits out their water.

"Well, your guarantee is crap! I wouldn't eat this garbage for the world!" The man's toupee flips backward as the crowd gasps in unison at his comments.

Suga gasps and shakes the hapless officer off her again, she slams down the tainted meat and grabs a spoonful of food she was preparing. She makes a beeline for the inspector who is turning colors arguing with Pook and Tanya. He happens to see her at the last-minute charging at him.

"Oh, heavens no!" He tries to scoot past the counter to escape, "Officers! Help!"

The officers look over too late as Suga bounces people out of her way. He is almost at the door when she grabs his jacket and spins him around to his knees.

"Officers! Halp!" He screams as patrons stand in their way.

"NO GARBAGE!" Suga bellows.

She tips back his head and opens his mouth to pour the food down his throat to his shock and dismay as he swallows helpless. She massages his neck to make sure he gulps it down. Food pours down his chin as he gargles.

"That's Zeke's justice!" Moe bellows.

Officers finally get past them to subdue Suga, she bats them off easily until one Tasers her. She grunts and let's go of the inspector's neck who drops to his hands and knees coughing and gagging. They must Tase her again to finally subdue her. Everyone is shooting cell phone video.

Tyrone happens to stumble out of the restroom, "Great Googly, man I feel a hundred twenty pounds lighter, I wouldn't use that restroom for about an hour." He pauses, notices the inspector on the floor, sauce smeared on his face and lips, the officers holding back the crowd, Suga drooling as she is being led out in shackles, the place in chaos.

"What'd I miss?"

Eat@Zeke's
Part VIII:
Ponyi Seen

Dayton

"Excuse me? How old is he? OMG!" Maureen blurts out loud into her cousins Chaps iPhone.

He rubs his ears. "Girl! Lower it down a notch!"

Silvia darts her eyes off from I-75 to glare over at her sister, "What? What'd he say? How old?"

Maureen holds up her hand, waves her away, "Heifer! Pay attention to the dang road, I got this!"

"Ha, you heifers are on I-75 also! Big D, little D!"

Silvia swerves, darts the mini Ford around a pothole, and looks at her sister again frowning.

Maureen growls, points two fingers at the road, "Focus girl! Focus your eyes inside the dang Focus! Detroit already sports sinkholes that will swallow up cars!"

"Swallows up, say what?" Chaps blurts into the phone.

"Chaps, relax, it wasn't what you're thinking! Go back to what you were saying. What happened when Joynae met Silva's -so-called 'internet boyfriend'?

"Girl, let me tell you, that Lil boy had mad game, I see how he pulled lil' vulnerable Silvas heart right out of her chest!"

"Oh snap, how little? Come on now, spill the beans!"

"Listen, okay, so Joynae got cuz Silva's voice down pat and last night convinced lil' Rerun to go downtown Dayton and have dinner with her at this plush lil' dive called Third Perk, they gots coffee and wine and all but, and ooh um, lemme tell you about the Creole Ribeye's, Mama would be proud, uh huh..."

"Chaps! The boy!"

"Oh right, okay so Joynae got lil backside just like Silv's but not her funny looking mug..." Maureen snickers as Silvia glances over curiously. "Anyways, so girl, Joynae's at the wine bar waiting on lil' Gary Coleman, we knows he's going to have on a Polo shirt and Timbs while carrying a white rose. I'm hiding out at a back table while she has her backside all poppin fresh all over the place causing a traffic jam in the restaurant you know what I'm saying. So, we are looking for this man and then walks in, a boy, a dang tween, maybe, twelve, thirteen?"

"How old? Oh, darling!" Maureen gasps.

Silvia swerves again disoriented.

"Girl he was pimping it too, ill Kangol pulled back, Pelle Pelle'd out, Gucci rope with the Timbs and Polo on, killing it for Junior high!"

Maureen shakes her head, "Dang! For real?"

"This lil boy strode like he done owned the store, ninety degrees lean, poppin and locking, oozing swag all over the place! I see how he got past security, they were confused!"

"What Joynae say to him??"

"Girl, I'm getting there, let me tell you! Joy put it on him! He approached, all swagerific, ready, thirsty! Lil' boy had the nerve to lick his lips when he spotted the booty, girl, it was horrible!"

"What she do??"

"All he got was "Silvia?" And it was on! She turned around slowly, glared at him - you should have seen his face, his jaw dropped, and his demeanor just all changed up. Joynae pointed her finger and snapped, "I got your Silvia boy! Boy you trying to catfish my ll cuz, wait, wait a minute, Tremel? Tremel Bishop? You were in my science class when I substituted at the prep academy! What! I should tan your hide over my knee you messing with the wrong fam! What's wrong with this picture? I know your Mama!"

Maureen starts clutching her sides trying not to laugh too hard.

"Girl, the whole joint was rolling, even the singer Brandon Harvey and the band Top Secret had to pause the jams to see what what up! Joynae was still cursing him out as he and his crew ran out of the place, oh and trust, I have that on my phone, watch, I'll send you the link to the upload!"

"Oh girl, that is nuts! I can't even hold it! I have to pee! Goodness, why does Zeke's keep calling this phone?

Silvia scrunches her face, "Well it's my phone that's why! They probably want to know where the bread order is, I'll get back with them later."

"Cougar, they call back to back. Pedophile."

"What? Pedophile? Cougar?"

"Honey child, handle your business, I'm trying to walk these dogs and I think they just spotted a muskrat! Cujo slow down!" Chaps blurt out.

"Boy, a muskrat?? Where are you with those crazy dogs?"

"I'm out in the Glen, they bout to yank me down these long and dank steps and I'm not the one!"

"Oh, Glen Helen? That pretty place with all the big trees and waterfalls and stuff we went to when we were kids? Aww, I like that place."

"Well drag your honey butt down here sometime and get your nature on, right now I'm bout to flip down these slippery steps, I gotta go bye!" Maureen hears yapping dogs losing their mind before Chaps disappears off the phone.

Casstown

"We here." Silvia brings Maureen to reality as they have left the highway and are driving through a Cass

Corridor neighborhood. Maureen rolls up her window. "What's the matter with you, you scared?" Silvia snickers.

"Girl, I had nightmares about this neighborhood since we were kids. I don't like coming over here."

"Nightmares? This neighborhood bout as hood as any other Detroit area. What's so different? Heck, I like some of the music shows I've seen down here."

Maureen looks at her solemnly, "Girl, you know this is the last place daddy was before he died. I think he saw the Rouge."

Silvia arches her eyebrow, "Say what? The what?"

"Girl, the Nain Rouge, didn't you ever hear that horror story when you were younger?" Maureen barely registers above a whisper prompting Silvia some concern. "When people see the lil' evil gnome-like character something bad happens to you. People have died, or got really sick, had war, lost their fortunes. Probably why Detroit bankrupt now! Daddy was down here getting flour for the restaurant right there around the corner, next thing you know he had the heart attack. I don't mess with this neighborhood."

"You really serious bout this, what is this, an urban legend of some sort? Oh, my goodness, Maureen believes in fairy tales?"

"Girl bye, I have to remember you the baby and they didn't share these stories with you. Let's find this Ponyi character, see what Kevin's got himself into, and get out!" Maureen's eyes open wide as she sulks down in the seat.

"And we need to discuss this intel that Chaps shared so eloquently with you." Silvia hisses before spotting the huge banner portraying 'Nain for Manager' in an announcement of the Marche du Nain Rouge parade.

Silvia shakes her head, "Wow, and I thought you were the only loony one."

They pull down a nondescript but busy neighborhood street, children are playing, and people are outside barbecuing, tending yards, and hanging laundry in this mostly working-class mixed cultural area. A carload of men slowly drive by blasting music and stare at the girls as they approach a small house set back from the road. An older car on blocks hogs the small driveway, hanging laundry cloaks the entranceway.

The phone buzzes again, Maureen holds it up to show twenty-two missed messages. Silvia shakes her head. Maureen turns it off and hands it to Silvia.

"And what are we doing here again? Darling, this doesn't look promising." Maureen surmises as Silvia climbs out of the car.

"Sis, let's go, we didn't come out here for nothing. This girl may know something, anything about where our brother has been for what, nine years? We owe this to Mama if anything, I would hate if something..."

"Shut it! Nothing's going to happen to Mother besides getting better - right? Let's go."

Maureen dons her Louis Vuitton bug glasses, sprays some Allure perfume on her Versace leather coat making sure she's fabulous arriving at the home. Silvia looks down to earth in her Apple Bottoms outfit as neighbors notice their stroll in tandem towards the door.

A petite Indian woman, in a traditional multicultural shawl, arrives on the small porch carrying a small basket of laundry. Maureen and Silvia stop short of the porch taking in the small woman as she does the same to them. Even doing domestic chores the young woman looks graceful, classy makeup applied, hair done back.

"May I help you?" She looks at them quizzically. "I don't talk to solicitors, you go up the street, no thank you."

The sisters' eye each other sassily, "Excuse me? Anyways baby girl are you Ponyi? Ponyi Patel?" Maureen breaks the ice.

"It's Pon-YI, like Ponzi without the Z, and not Pony-i like the stupid animal. Ba-Be girl, you sound like you're making a pitch that I'm not buying. So, who wants to know, I've paid my taxes, my bills are up..."

"Girl, this isn't about you. We're not collecting any money or nothing. We're looking for somebody you may know..." Silvia injects.

Ponyi arches her back and gets a look of defiance on her face before starting to retreat to the house, "I don't know anybody, and I'm not from here. Please go."

"Ponyi, please, it's our brother. Kevin, Kevin Woods. We've been looking for him a long time. Please."

She pauses hearing his name before continuing opening the door.

Maureen steps forward, "Wait, I'm not sure what your relationship is with our brother but you have to understand, we love him and he left us under bad circumstances. We're not intending any harm to him if you're trying to protect him. We miss him dearly and you seem to be the only connection to him after our mother cho...choked your name out on her hospital bed..." Maureen is not able to continue.

Ponyi grips the door, stoic in her stance until she hangs her head.

Maureen turns, not able to face them, she grips the laundry pole line. Silvia takes a breath and steps forward, "Ponyi, our mother is sick, possibly dying, she has not said a word in the last two days - until she said your name, who we've never ever heard of. Please help us."

The women are at a standstill as silence envelopes the chaotic yard. Not even the busy neighborhood could be heard. Maureen takes a breath and wipes her face. The next person who sobs is Ponyi. Silvia and Maureen eye each other and take the cue to approach her.

"Ponyi sweetie, please." Silvia touches her shoulder.

The confronted woman looks up, her makeup smeared, her face softened. Maureen takes the basket. "I know who you are Woods sisters. I am sorry, this is very difficult for me to retain this secrecy, and this has never been my intent."

They sit on a bench on the porch, "Secrecy? What is going on Ponyi, were you dating my brother? It's okay, you can tell us. We just need to know where he is!"

Ponyi hangs her head lower as the girls try to comfort her. "It's okay Ponyi, we just want to contact him, for our mother."

"He doesn't think we blame him for what happened to our dad, does he? That is so not the case if it is." Silvia blurts out as even Maureen eyes her surprised.

"You two are nice, your brother spoke highly of you. Sorry to come all this way and I am no help. For you see, your brother, I have not seen him in a long time, my apologies."

"Wait, really? I mean, do you have his number, email, anything to contact him?"

Ponyi shakes her head, children laughing, coming closer interrupts their moment. She gets her wits about herself and stands, "Listen, it was nice meeting you two, I had hoped to meet his family would have been under better circumstances, give my regards to your mother, she is an outstanding woman, hate to hear of her illness. I must go."

Maureen starts to become unravelled, stands, "OMG, Silvia, I knew this was a dead end, this whole situation with Mama and Kevin, this neighborhood, this is getting to me sis! I feel i'm getting the hives! Come!"

The children become louder as Ponyi nervously tries to get her basket into the house, "I must go, good day Woods sisters."

"Wait, what, what is happening? Ponyi please." Silvia attempts to walk into the house with her much to Ponyi's surprise.

"Please Sissy, let's go! I feel the Nain Rouge is here!" Maureen is escaping halfway across the yard tripping over children's toys.

Ponyi pushes on the door, "Ms. Woods, please! Go!"

Silvia, taller than the short Indian suddenly notices something odd on the adjoining bookshelf. She stiffens, quiets as Ponyi follows her gaze. Her pupils widen, she bites her lip as the two women eye each other.

"Ponyi, is that?"

Ponyi shakes her head, "No, no, please, do not go there."

"Oh my goodness!" Silvia's mouth drops as she whips out her phone, she turns it on and searches for a number.

"No, it's not what you think, Ms. Woods, please! I beg of you!" Ponyi pleads to deaf ears as Silvia heads off the porch.

Maureen, almost at the car but trying to avoid a bicycle notices Silvia all smiles, "Heifer, what in the world? What happened? Who are you calling?"

"Ugh! They are still calling crazy from the restaurant!" Silvia puts her finger up as Maureen curls her lip. "I'm calling my homegirl Layne Weiss, she's a journalist."

Ponyi puts her face into her hands.

"Excuse me?"

"Layne? Hey girl, hey. What are you doing?"

Layne is surrounded by thumping music and lots of chatter, "Living the dream girl, about to interview Slum Village up at the Fillmore. What's good, how's Mama?"

"She's the same girl, still on critical. Hoping for the best."

"Sorry baby, I'm hoping too."

"Slum Village huh? That's your boys, how are they doing?"

"I know right, they doing it big up here with Guilty Simpson and Black Milk, I'm in heaven right now. Interviewing all of them!"

"Oh, I'm jealous! Need to take me next time!"

"Nothing but a thing to call me, you know where I am."

"No doubt, speaking of which, what's the word on Kommandoz performing here? I remember you interviewed them some time also. Aren't they coming soon?"

"Kommandoz? Oh yeah, Utopia already copped tickets from me for their show. They're here this weekend."

"Oh goodness, that is wonderful! Layne, you ever talk with their drummer?" Silvia searches her phone for pictures of the band.

"Their drummer? Kwame? You know, I've talked with everybody in the crew, but he seems to never be available. Odd, he's the D-town native too."

"Wait, did you say Kwame? Is that the right name?"

Ponyi sits down, sobs on the porch.

"Yeah, the last article I posted his name Kwame Da' man, girl you know that's probably his stage name. Why?"

Silvia gasps while looking at an obscure side view picture of Kwame looking nutty.

"Silvia?" Both Layne and Maureen ask her quizzically.

"Layne girl, I know you busy, thanks baby girl. I'll be reading your Inmylanye.com when I get home!"

"Oh okay girl, had me worried. You do that and make sure to get me some of that great Ten-cheese Soul macaroni, I've been craving it! Hit me up you need anything!"

"Okay girl, hook me up for that show and I'll bring you all the cheesy mac you want!"

"Done!"

Silvia hangs up the phone and approaches Maureen trying to get her heel out of the bicycle spokes. "Baby girl, what was all that? Said this place was getting under my skin - so this better be good." Silvia eyes her with a weird smile, a mild look of shock. Maureen looks at her concerned, "Wait, what, what is it?"

Silvia holds up her phone to show the picture of the drummer, Maureen's eyes go wide.

Their moment is interrupted by children running into the yard. The children are laughing, running, kicking a ball back and forth. They range in age from seven to nine, two of them are little Hispanic boys, one white, two black, the middle child is distinctively black but with a reddish tint and wavy curls.

This boy slows, eyes the women curiously. Maureen and Silvia stand rigid, startled, their gut feeling was one of familiarity.

The boy's friends look on unaware their friend's predicament.

"Hey Kevin, see you at school!" The boys race off to their respective homes for lunch.

Silvia drops her phone as Maureen's mouth gapes. The wedged bicycle suddenly falls off her foot.

Ponyi sighs, "Kevin, say hi to your aunts and come eat your lunch." He waves at them as they meekly wave back. He races off into his home hugging his mother before entering.

Ponyi shrugs, "We'll talk."

“Mommy, which aunts are those?”

“Kevin, do you remember anything about your father…?” Before she closes the door.

The sisters nod speechless.

Eat@Zeke's
Pt. IX:
Flapjacks

Fluffy Flapjacks

2 cups all-purpose flour
3 tablespoons white sugar
2 teaspoons baking powder
1 teaspoon baking soda
1/2 teaspoon salt
2 cups milk
2 eggs
1/4 cup canola oil
cooking spray

Whisk flour, sugar, baking powder, baking soda, and salt together in a bowl until no lumps remain. Add milk, eggs, and oil; whisk until batter is runny and well mixed.

Heat a non-stick griddle over medium heat and lightly spray with cooking spray. Pour in a portion of the batter. Cook until bubbles form, 3 to 4 minutes. Turn and cook, pressing middle gently with the spatula, until lightly browned on the other side, 2 to 3 minutes more. Repeat with the remaining batter.

If you don't like something, change it. If you can't change it, change your attitude.

Maya Angelou

Detroit

"Get your flapjacks here! Get your flapjacks!" Zeke's Kitchen is seemingly back open, well sort of. The temporary vendors entice passer-byes with their tasty entrees, yelling specials of the day, seducing you with their delicious smells, large exciting visuals drawing you in. It's a sight to see in-route to work.

Still closed, Zeke's Kitchen, the building, sits idle as the favorite west side restaurant has been overrun by barbeque pits, sandwich carts, hot dog stands, and the omnipresent food trucks. Friends, associates, and so-called Zeke Fanatics are all lending their support and service in an unprecedented effort to 'Occupy Zeke's' in the famous restaurant's time of peril.

By occupying the parking lot of the shuttered enterprise, the vendors are supporting the cause started by disgruntled patrons who learned their favorite cafe was closed by what they claim is a 'conspiracy."

Their chants of 'Eat at Zeke's', 'Eat at Zeke's, 'Eat at Zeke's' coupled with the parking lot frenzy has caught the city's attention.

"Mama, that sweet dear woman is a legacy in this community. Mama and Zeke, I grew up craving their delicacies, the succulent yams, the fresh turnip greens..."

"Turn it up!" A kid yells.

"As I was saying, the Chicken Fried Steak, the Black-Eyed Peas, Okra, collard greens, fried fish, and heck even all the Pigs Feet, Ribs. Mama makes them dripping off the bone so-so good... What's that? Am I worried about the fat content? Heck no, not with Mama, they hooked up their food lean, low fat. Trust Mama know how to cook! I'm trying to be slick like her!" Carlton flips a flapjack, "So you ordering from me? How much you want?" Carlton chuckles and keeps working.

The crowd surrounding Zeke's has swelled to capacity in an unprecedented show of support for a fallen local hero. It's standing room only as the local neighborhood and Zeke's fanatics have descended on the parking lot shouting, "Eat at Zeke's" in unison. As officials were alerted to the burgeoning scene, it's surprisingly primary peaceful crowd with just the chants and sounds of vendors promoting their wares. It is a fitting testament to the woman who many thinks of as a surrogate mother.

"Be sure to get your nice watch, got your nice watch here! I know you want one, I know you do." Stephen yells from his cart.

'Occupy Zeke's' has morphed into a political movement as the peaceful protesters lament against a political system they feel is designed for failure against small business owners, especially against African-Americans.

Operating for years in the backdrop of the auto industry, Zeke's Kitchen thrived serving factory workers and the surrounding neighborhoods southern soul food delicacies. As many of the workers were new arrivals in the north seeking work amidst the civil rights movement. A touch of home was highly appreciated.

Freddy Styles runs the nearby community center and is a long-time family friend. "See, the magnitude of the unification of all adopted parties, rallying in support against the unseen oppressor is a positive thing. By taking a systematic tranquil approach the people are taking a nod from the forefathers who worked the lunch counters, who skipped the bus, who marched on the capital, who laid the foundation, deep in the trenches, crawling under barbed wire, escaping mortar shells, plugging the bleeding holes with your bare thumb, spotting the curve of their eyes hiding in the brush..."

"Sir, are you referring to the Vietnam War or Civil Rights movement?" A puzzled lady asks.

Freddy scoffs, ponders over his mistake, "I digress, ma'am, it was a trying time of change for us all. Let us savor the current situation."

"Savor? Savor this Diablo Dog!" A vendor from Zombie Dogz hot dog food truck blurts out holding a huge turkey Diablo with all the fixings.

"Diablo Dog? A devil dog? The savior has been insulted! Where's the justice for the king?" An elderly passer-by injects into the conversation.

"Hey bro it's just food, man, chill. Just say your blessings before you eat, and you'll be alright." The vendor shakes his head.

Preacher Man from the local Heavenly Righteous Missionary Baptist church Mama attends suddenly appears and touches the food box, "I pray in Jesus name the sanctity and blessings of this fine food presented to us on this fateful day, and for all the love and support given to Mama in her time of need. In his glorious name, Amen!" The vendor smirks and lets the hungry preacher take the food.

The preacher takes one bite as he juggles a flapjack in his hand, he drops the hot dog onto the flapjack. He shrugs and wraps the dog in the flapjack. Hmm, tastes good.

"Preacher Man is eating the diablo!" A passer-by gasps.

"And I have rid it of all its evil misrepresentation, cleared it of its evil spirit, sanctified it in the glory of good to be consumed, by myself, in its entirety and it is delicious."

"I just saw lighting come out the preachers' fingers cleansing that Diablo dog!" A kid quips.

Curious folks bump Preacher Man trying to eat, he scoffs, "Lord have mercy, folks, there is enough bounty to share, remember, we are here to support Ms. Woods!"

The crowd fills to capacity milling around the food trucks, curious to what is happening with Preacher Man. So much that his branded flapjack flips out of his grip.

Big Moe, Zach, and Quinton Jones navigate the crowd as the larger gentleman can move through easier leaving his buddies able to follow in the wake.

Quinton stays on his iPhone navigating his daily hustle. Zach keeps close to his boys in the swelling crowd. "Figure out what are we going to eat?" Zach asks anxiously.

"Why, you getting nervous, white boy?" Quinton smirks

"Naw bruh, I'm cool, my stomach is growling and its mad hot up in here, black folks sweating!"

Moe chuckles, "It is hot, and Moe is hungry!"

"They have that chicken and waffles cart set up Moe?" Quinton can barely see overhead.

"Not confirmed Q, Moe needs food!"

"Yo Big M, why you talk about yourself in third person homie?" Zach innocently ponders. Moe looks down at his hesitating friend, nostrils flared.

A curious child, maybe eleven, reaches out through the swelling crowd, his mother distracted with his younger brothers and sisters. The child almost being stepped on as feet trample around the generic Styrofoam plate amongst the destroyed grass. His fingers stretch, fondle the edge of the recycled material, pulls it forward. He grips Preacher Man's flapjack and his eyes go wide as he looks at it closely. The crowd pushes and pulls around him as he stands still, mesmerized, in a trance.

His mother Adanna finally notices, tugs at him. "Ebele, come, it is getting too wild here, let us go." Her voice concerned, she is from West Africa, her husband, a U.S. Soldier.

A woman glances over his shoulder, eyes go wide, she shrieks, "Its Jesus! It's the savior in the flapjack!"

The immediate crowd surges forward, as gasps and shocked groans inspect the burnt dough.

A man shakes, yells out, "Jesus is real! He has blessed Mama in the flapjack!"

The crowd surges again, Adanna is nervous for her children as the open air grows dimmer.

"They saw Jesus in a flapjack!" It was spreading.

"Jesus has spoken from the flapjack!" The word was getting twisted.

"The flapjack heals you!" The gossip waned downhill.

"Heal me Jesus!" Somebody reaches, another person falls, the swelling murmur opens into a full-fledged roar.

Adanna clings desperately onto her children as the crowd morphs into a pack reaching and grabbing for the flapjack.

As quickly as it became, the crowd suddenly parts like the Red Sea. The boy and his family are scooped up like pawns discarded after a bad chess game.

Big Moe bellows, "Leave them alone! Big Moe got them!" He moves them towards the side away from the following crowd.

"Ebele, discard the pancake, let somebody else carry it." Adanna looks down to where he was, he is gone.

"Where the lil' dude go?" Zach trips out.

"Ebele! No! Come back!" His mother cries.

"There he goes! He has Jesus!" Somebody cries out.

"Get him!"

The frightened Ebele grips the flapjack and crashes into a cart flipping it over, angry businessmen yell at him. The chase is on.

"People! Keep calm! This is nonsense!" Freddy Styles yells over a loudspeaker as the crowd chases the boy.

Frightened, Ebele slips between people and knocks over items in his haste as the local Detroit's finest take notice.

Moe looks Adanna in her eye, "I promise, I will retrieve your boy, what is his name?"

Her teeth chattering, "Ebele"

"I will bring back Ebele I promise!" Moe rears up to move through the crowd.

The officer calls out, "Hey boy, what you got there?" He touches his shoulder, Ebele jerks not realizing who it was.

The officer puts his hand on his baton but Ebele backs off, "Relax, I am an officer of the law. Son, you take something, what did you take? Come here."

Ebele, disoriented, sees the pale tall slender officer motioning for him, he turns to see the mob coming in his direction. In his confusion, he runs.

"Hey, I said stop!" The officer calls it in and goes in pursuit.

The crowd looks in confusion as the cop sprints past and sirens are heard in the distance as the crowd turns ugly. Camera phones click away recording everything.

The tree line twists upside down, the heat emanates off the hot pavement, the air is stiff as people scream and shout. Wails of sirens erupt from everywhere, even among all the confusion all Ebele could hear was his breath and heartbeat.

"I said stop in the name of the law!' A click of a gun is heard. Time stands still.

The officer looks directly at Big Moe standing in his way.

"Dear Officer John Doe, I believe by you confronting the young man, startling him in his disorientation, touching him inappropriately, you violated the law by assault. By not having all the facts presented to you, you reacted by your survival instincts. Now not by a normal human, but the heightened insecurity those officers bring to the job with them. Every little twitch, every little reach, anything out of the ordinary you must be conscious too. It's understandable in your choice of professions and I don't envy your position. From the same standpoint as you; the oppressor's mistrust of the community, especially us as African-Americans you displace blame. A bullet does not have a soul, its victims are chosen by those who hold the power, and once in flight the oppressor who squeezed the trigger can displace his conscious. And we, as the oppressed must comply, whether we agree or not, or we suffer the consequences, jailed, beaten, killed, a life destroyed, entire families destroyed. We have but a few seconds to make this choice, to stand up for what we feel is an injustice, being targeted for something silly, something simple and insignificant or it could be something more serious, a theft, a pocket of drugs, yes, a crime could have been committed but in these mere seconds is somebody's life worth it to die? Officer John Doe, take that moment of choice, past all your extensive training, our general distrust of each other, whatever anger is in your head against somebody different than you, and think, are you beyond human that you must take this person's life? Are they that much of a threat you must end his existence? This person does have a mother and a father, a family that cares for them, they could be a parent themselves, in school trying to better themselves, off work from a hard day - was it worth it? Before it's us versus them, before the day begins and whatever happens, we are all human, bleed and breathe the same way. Keep faith alive that there is a God looking over us and we all must pray for his forgiveness whatever religion you follow.

And my fellow African-Americans, Hispanics, Jewish, Arabs, Indians, whoever feels oppressed from the overseers we can do better by being better educated, being more knowledgeable about the laws, by being less confrontational - and I'm not saying bow down and not saying anything if you feel they are in the wrong - but by having more wisdom we play on their level. Challenge them intelligently. They have less reason to treat us as subhuman, as the oppressed, as less than man. If you are full of attitude and a chip on your shoulder, channel it into working to challenge the system productively, believe it or not, we have rights, use them."

The officer looks again as there is a solid wall of people standing between him and Ebele. Moe has been joined by Quinton, Zach, Freddy, Adanna, the food vendors, the mixed-race crowd supporting Zeke's Kitchen, supporting their neighborhood. It is deadly quiet as the police force looks into the eyes of the citizens, the citizens of Detroit, the citizens of the United States of America coming together.

Moco's father, policeman Scott Jones, places his hand on John's shoulder.

Officer John Doe puts his pistol down as his fellow officers look on surprised. Ebele emerges from the crowd holding the flapjack up, gives the officer the gift of Jesus.

DEDICATED TO MICHAEL BROWN, PHILANDO CASTILE, JOHN CRAWFORD, TAMIR RICE, SANDRA BLAND, TREVON MARTIN AND ALL OF THE OTHER NEEDLESS KILLINGS IN THE NAME OF THE LAW SINCE 1476

Elsewhere…

Smoke filters, fluffs, dissipates over burnt flapjacks sizzling in the forgotten about skillet, shrivelled three quarters to the size they normally would be. Dwele plays in the background crooning about the flavored pastries. An iPhone buzzes on the counter, inches slightly towards a turned over bottle of syrup dripping slowly. The text is from Silvia and Maureen. "Girl we heard you have tickets to the Kommandoz concert! We need to go with you to turn it up! We have a surprise for you!"

Children play in the backyard, laughing, yelling happily, oblivious to the underlying drama.

Utopia stands by the pool, distraught, staring into space. Her fingers part as she drops a letter by her side, her world is crushed.

Eat@Zeke's
Part X:
Burnt Gizzards

Southern Fried Chicken Gizzards

1-pound chicken gizzards, rinsed
2 stalks celery, cut into chunks
1 onion, cut into chunks
2 bay leaves
1 1/2 teaspoons celery salt, divided
1 teaspoon seasoned salt
1/2 teaspoon ground black pepper
1/2 teaspoon dried Italian herb seasoning
1 teaspoon garlic powder
1/4 teaspoon ground cumin
1/2 teaspoon Louisiana-style hot sauce
3 cups oil for deep frying
1 cup all-purpose flour

Place the chicken gizzards, celery, onion, bay leaves, and 1 teaspoon of celery salt into a saucepan, and pour in enough water to cover the gizzards by 1 inch. Bring the gizzards to a boil, reduce heat to low, cover, and simmer until tender, about 2 1/2 hours. Pour in more water during simmering, if needed, to keep gizzards covered. Remove the gizzards to a bowl, discard the celery and onion, and reserve the broth.

Season with 1/2 teaspoon of celery salt, seasoned salt, pepper, Italian seasoning, garlic powder, cumin, and hot sauce, stirring well. Pour 1/3 cup of the reserved broth over the seasoned gizzards, and refrigerate for 30 minutes, stirring often. Heat oil in a deep-fryer or large saucepan to 375 degrees F (190 degrees C).

Place the flour in a plastic bag and pour in the gizzards with their seasoning. Shake the bag to thoroughly coat the gizzards with flour. Gently lower about 1/4 of the gizzards per batch into the hot oil, and fry until golden brown, about 5 minutes per batch. Drain the gizzards on paper towels and serve hot.

Detroit

The huge fire lights up the Detroit night sky with crimson red, amber orange, vibrant yellow, and brilliant blue.

Flashing red and blue lights race through the dark city streets, fueling hope to quell the towering blaze. The lights cast ominous shadows as they bounce inside previous burnt-out shells of the cities former glorious neighborhoods. Waffling black smoke dances in the strobe-lights creeping up to the full moon.

Zeke's Kitchen was burning.

Remaining residents wander out of their homes dumbfounded, flabbergasted in pajamas and robes as they soak up the scene. Standing, starring, perplexed, in disbelief of what they are witnessing.

An elderly woman, who's been a patron of Zeke's for over thirty years pulls her shawl over her neck. She stands near a younger family. The younger boy notices a single tear on her cheek.

She takes a deep breath, exhales, "Smells like waffles."

"I smell sweet potato pie, or maybe its candied yams. It's no matter." Another man inhales.

A woman slows down in her car, "Oh my goodness, I can taste the cheesiest mac and cheese. I want some."

Tyrone Hill stumbles out of his hole, he drops a liquor bottle and falls to his knees, he places his hat over his chest. Taking a deep breath, he starts to sing,

"The colors of the rainbow so pretty in the sky

Or also on the faces of people going by

I see friends shaking hands, saying "How do you do?"

They're really saying, I love you

I hear babies crying, I watch them grow

They'll learn much more and I'll never know

And I think to myself

What a wonderful life..."

~Louis Armstrong

The swelling crowd stays quiet listening to the stirring but odd acapella rendition.

"Mmmmm collard greens, black-eyed peas. Oh, I'm weak fellas." Fire Chief Brian Scott groans at the site as he steps out of the cab of the truck. "Let's put this blaze out now men! Save the food!"

"Man, this was the food we had catered at my wedding! Remember you D'jayed at it Chief. We have to save this joint!" His second in command bellows as he attaches the hoses.

"Let's use the good equipment, we can't hold back for this one no matter the costs. The city council can kiss my butt! Let's go!"

"We'll just add it to the cities bankruptcy!"

They smile, and both show their wristbands of "Eat@Zekes", nodding in agreement before rushing towards the blaze with their team.

The shameless food cart operators arrive opening their business for the growing crowd.

Embers dance and spiral into the night sky floating upwards as the city mourns another lost icon. Somewhere a little devilish imp chuckles and skips away into the mist gleefully.

Fox Theatre

Silvia bumps between people in the crowded theatre making her way to her seat. Her cell is buzzing constantly but she can't answer it quickly enough. Utopia and Sasha await in their aisle. Utopia is distant, distraught, and quiet as her friend attempts to cheer her up.

"Utopia, really, what's up? You've been quiet since we picked you up. What happened since the last time we talked?"

Utopia shrugs, "Don't worry about it. Enjoy the show, Black Milk is on next."

Silvia squeezes by, her phone still erupting. "Is Mo back?"

"Get your cell, nothing more annoying than somebody ignoring important information." Utopia snarls.

"Girl, what's eating you? I'll get it, dang."

"She got something up her butt, I don't know, she's been like this all evening."

"Stop riding my back Sasha, jeez. Sil, why did you and Mo want to come here so badly for anyway? You - you're more a Maxwell, Kem type, and Maureen is ol' school."

"You are foul tonight lil' Miss. And I'm down with Black Milk, Slum, Dilla, Apollo and Guilty, Common, Lupe, Kid Cudi. In fact, we may be meeting a special member of Kommandoz tonight."

"Oh really, how you figure? You a groupie now or something? I know you're not being a thot, mama would awake from her coma."

"Hey, watch it young miss. Mama is not in any coma. What's your deal?" Maureen arrives with drinks. Silvia finally answers her cell.

Sasha shakes her head while taking a drink, "Some message she received today got her all in her feelings."

"Watch the show, lights are dimming." Utopia bites.

Silvia drops her cell in the dark. The girls look at her concerned as she shakes. Black Milk is starting his show, but they don't hear him. The bass vibrates through them, flipping their stomachs.

Maureen grabs her arm, "Sil, what's the deal?"

Trembling Silvia picks the cell back up, covers her ear, "What, say that again? I don't understand, I was just there. I just checked up on the restaurant, made sure everything was okay after the protest. We were just there."

Maureen looks into her eye pleading, "Silvia, what is happening? I can barely hear anything."

Silvia puts up her finger, "This was after everybody had left? Did somebody get shot running away from the scene? Do they know who it was? This is too much."

Sasha and Utopia look at her mortified, "What the what is happening Silvia?"

Silvia sighs and shuts off her cell, rubs her face before turning to them, tears continue to flow. "Zeke's is on fire. Our restaurant is on fire." Their mouths drop.

The eccentric hard bass snaps back in as the four of them are lost in their own world.

Detroit City Distillery

Theodore and Marty Simon cheer with a bottle of Detroit City Vodka along with City Commissioner Marisol Banter at a secluded booth in the corner. Outside a familiar BMW arrives.

Ezekiel walks past a live newsreel of the restaurant burning as he joins his partners. "Adios partners, heard we have a breakthrough with the development deal. Ms. Banter, good to see you again." Ezekiel kisses her hand and winks at her.

"Likewise," She blushes, the men look as if there is more to the wink and the smile.

"Word has it your mother is out of the Woods." Theodore quips as Ezekiel squints his eyes at him. Marty shakes his head.

"My mother is still in a doctor-induced coma mind you Mr. Simon, I have no need and no mood for your lackadaisical stabs at humor especially where it concerns my family." Ezekiel stares Theodore right in the eye making his elder partner squirm.

The waitress brings Ezekiel a glass as Theodore stutters an uncomfortable apology, "Well, no need to get snotty ol' boy. Was genuinely concerned about your mother is all. No harm."

"No worries Theodore ol' boy." Ezekiel gives him a smirk as they raise their glasses in a toast.

Marty sighs a sigh of relief, elated to avoid a potential heated meltdown, "To new development and new beginnings, Ezekiel without your knowledge and research this project wouldn't have seen the light of day. Kudos my esteemed partner, you've done Detroit proud."

Ezekiel swishes the local concoction and grins, "Thank you, Marty, I'm just a small pawn in the game. Just looking to elevate our small fledgling partnership with our quality clients." He raises his glass towards Ms. Banter, she smiles.

"To you and your Zekey." The Simon brothers eye each other curiously mouthing 'Zekey?' She continues, "The city is grateful your firm has been instrumental in clearing up red tape and opening up new opportunities. It's necessary baby steps to bring back the city." They tap and sip, she brushes his foot with hers. "And bringing back fond memories." She smiles at him. "Speaking of which isn't Mo in town? How's that working out for you?" She pauses senses his losing interest, she adds, "Does *she* know she's here?" He snaps his head glaring at her, nostrils flaring.

Theodore perks up, "Well, Zekey boy, you ready to meet our silent partner? Tonight's the night we've talked about. He just informed me he's here."

"Theodore, we've been partners now seven years, you may call me Mr. Woods."

Theodore slants his eyes not expecting that response, he glances over at Marisol who shrugs nonchalantly. Marty raises his glass, "Been a long time coming Ezekiel, but since the recent victory of our success, our silent partner agreed to finally meet with us tonight. He's been very instrumental in acquiring data and more importantly, the funding to assist the partners purchasing parcels and making the project come to life!"

Ezekiel finally breaks his gaze at Theodore and Marisol, wipes his mouth with a napkin and looks around, "Okay, I'm game, been curious about this connection for months. We needed funding, he came through. Who can we thank for this?"

"Me fool, P.I.M.P. I told you I was going to collect on that old blood arrangement one day. You're welcome." Lydell Winkelman leans on his cane directly behind him smirking.

Ezekiel almost spits out his vodka. He sits up glaring at Lydell, then his partners. "Surely you're kidding me? This is some type of prank? Am I on "Punked?"

Theo and Marty look perplexed, "Ezekiel, Mr. Winkelman comes highly recommended, an astute businessman. Was able to make many negotiations right for us."

"And of course, he insisted on keeping it in secrecy." Ezekiel shakes his head.

"Zekey ol' boy, said you two went to school together. Played on the same teams. Figured you'd be okay." Theo quips making the situation worse.

"I got your Zekey damn it."

"Ezekiel, you know Lydell has worked with the planning commission, he's very instrumental in the city's redevelopment. I am surprised at your tone." Marisol looks on seriously.

"This is absurd. Obviously, my partner's blinders are strong. This poses a serious dilemma! What seriously did you foresee the outcome of this collaboration?"

Lydell brushes his pointy goatee, smirks as he glances over to the television and back, "Payback's a bitch isn't it Zekey? Oh, gentrification doesn't necessarily have to be an evil word, but in the hands of the hood's chosen son it's going to be quite ugly isn't it?"

Marisol follows Lydell's gaze to the breaking news events, she gasps. "Oh, my goodness, Ezekiel isn't that your mother's restaurant?"

Ezekiel breaks his gaze from Lydell, his eyes resting on the live news report from the burning restaurant. Mouth agape, he is truly shaken, wobbly, he was standing, and he now must sit.

Lydell cackles in the background ominously. "Probably that crazy fat cook got out of jail and burnt some collard greens pizza!"

Ezekiel leans forward, snatches the cane and rams it in Lydell's bad leg. Lydell groans in agony as his entourage rushes forward. "Fellas you come any closer and this hidden blade I know is in here, will completely displace Lie – Dell's remaining leg! Now sir - number one, I will never ever submit to doing business with a known criminal such as you. Number two, if you're sorry ass excuse for a man had anything to do with this fire… I swear to the heavens above you will meet your demise!"

"You're making a bad decision Wood's." Lydell sneers, gasping nervously.

"You sir are the bad decision! It's MR. WOOD'S to you!" He turns to the shocked table. "Don't ever bring this fool around to do business again or this whole firm is getting sued and no more partners. Trust! Good day!" Ezekiel drops the cane on Lydell's leg with a thud and storms out of the diner. Nobody stands in his way.

Fox Theatre

The hip-hop band Kommandoz are going through an energetic opening set that includes ukuleles, rattle shakers, Sambas, rattlers, bongo's and more as the eclectic group wraps up their set. The large ensemble rocks together in unison bringing their unique sound to life behind the energetic artists rapping to the groove.

Finishing off the set with one of their early reggae hybrid classics 'Believer'; the vibe is relaxed, calm, the lights are dimmed, and fans have their lighters and cell phones held high.

Silvia and Maureen push their way towards the front eager to see if their Intel about their long-lost brother was correct.

Kevin Woods was already seen as the outcast of the family over ten years ago, running in and out of trouble, hanging with the wrong crowd, dropping out of high school, catching minor felonies. He was on his way to becoming a statistic, another lost fallen soldier, succumbing to the pressures of the mean streets. Zeke Sr. had already shown him the front door disappointed in his young seed's choices. Mama always let him in through the back door to get a sandwich or cop a nap.

Things went to the head the night Zeke Sr. left this earth. As he was all the way across the city in Casstown getting supplies for his restaurant, he was filling his truck when allegedly he was jumped by juvenile delinquents. Three young teenagers allegedly were seen fleeing the scene as Zeke laid on the hard pavement clutching his heart. While not proven the he was shot or stabbed; alas he passed that evening.

One young man's pants were so low he lost them behind a bush as he scaled a fence. His school badge was in his pockets along with a 38' revolver tucked in his waistband. That teenager was Kevin's best friend Quinn. Shortly after Kevin was called in to be questioned, he vanished from the Motor City. Ezekiel Jr., his own older brother, declared his guilt and put a restraining order against him to never return to his family home. He even assisted the investigators in his search and recovery, not for the fam's sake, for his persecution. Nobody has heard from him since.

Mama and his sisters have tried in vain to locate him, to update him that charges had been dropped, that he was cleared of any wrongdoing. They have failed continuously. Now, a decade later Mama lies in the hospital, possibly on her deathbed, the family reunited around her side, the fate of their beloved restaurant up in smoke. All of Silvia and Maureen's research, along with the surprise twist of Kevin

Jr. living in their home city, has led them to this hip-hop show at the Fox Theatre.

As Silvia and Maureen flank the beefy security guard blocking the stage, their eyes gaze past the front men prancing back and forth, the plethora of musicians jamming their instruments, the smoke, and dimness of the arena, to the lone drummer backing up the band in the back. In the press this man's name is Kwame Da'Man, with a long strand of natty dreads bouncing over his eyes, a heavy chinstrap goatee complete with a beaded point, tattooed out, older, filled out, in shape, he looked good. This was not the same baby-faced, naive, didn't know a drumstick from a guitar pick. Kevin, they had last seen years ago with so much trouble on his mind. But, their gut instincts all pointed that this indeed was Kevin.

As the song fades and the group raises their fists in triumph they shout out, "Yo Detroit! Get ready for your native sons "Slum Village!" The crowd jumps into an uproar as T3, Illa J, and the Young RJ are joined by honorary member Elizhi to break into rhyme.

Elizhi calls out "Yo, What's up Detroit!' Much to the crowd's delight. "We want to start off the show giving mad props to a community institution and a favorite drop off stop of mine to get the one and only Collard Greens Pizza." The crowd whoops and hollers knowing what restaurant he's referring too. "Zeke's Kitchen Y'all." And they applaud in respect.

"The boys and I were going to stop by Zeke's tonight after Dilla's Delights to bash." People yell out 'Dilla' after mentioning the beloved supreme producer. "Instead we found a standoff amongst a protest." The crowd goes silent as several concur they were there. "It ended peacefully thanks to a divine intervention by God, thank goodness after so many similar recently haven't. Nobody's lives were lost." The crowd claps. "Regrettably afterward somebody caught the store on fire." The crowd gasps and there are people crying. "We going to rock this set to our beloved hometown, Zeke's Kitchen and Mama's speedy recovery that she'll be back to build. We need our Soul, we need our soul food!" They clap again in a roar as the backing band picks up the groove.

As the members of Slum Village start to rock they fail to notice a small but significant side-note happening to the left. As their tour-mate, Kommandoz drummer Kwame stares like a deer caught in headlights, his eyes watery, he drops his sticks. Blindsided, he stares face to face with his equally teary-eyed lost family.

News report

A channel 7 news reporter interviews the oddest person on the street outside Zeke's as Tyrone sings in the background. Akee, the gas station manager next door smiles for the camera hawking fake gold from his store. "Yo, I hear an explosion and felt the heat singe my goatee. I am not allowed to eat but I swear I smelt my favorite gizzards from Zeke's burning! I rushed out smelling burnt gizzards and my mouth dropped... It's a shame, a tragic shame..."

Eat@Zeke's
Part XI:
Government Cheese

Sea Salt Caramel Swirl Cheesecake Bars

1 1/2 cups graham cracker crumbs
3 tablespoons white sugar
6 tablespoons butter or margarine, melted
3 (8 ounce) packages cream cheese, softened
3/4 cup sugar
1/8 teaspoon salt
3 eggs
1 teaspoon vanilla extract
2 tablespoons light cream
1/2 teaspoon rum extract (optional)
1/2 cup walnut pieces (optional)
1 2/3 cups Sea Salt Caramel Baking Chips

Heat oven to 350 degrees F. Line 13x9x2-inch baking pan with foil, extending foil beyond pan sides. CRUMB CRUST: Stir together 1-1/2 cups graham cracker crumbs and 3 tablespoons sugar in medium bowl; blend in 6 tablespoons melted butter or margarine, mixing well. Press mixture onto bottom of baking pan. Beat cream cheese, sugar and salt in large bowl until smooth. Add eggs, one at a time, beating well after each addition. Stir in vanilla. Set aside 3-1/2 cups batter; blend light cream and rum extract into remaining batter. Stir in walnuts, if desired.

Place caramel chips in medium microwave-safe bowl. Microwave at MEDIUM (50%) 1 minute; stir. Until chips are melted and smooth when stirred. Gradually stir rum and nut batter into melted chips, stirring until well blended. Alternately drop vanilla batter and caramel nut batter by heaping tablespoons onto crumb crust. With knife or small spatula swirl batters for marbled effect. (Batters will flatten and smooth as cheesecake batter bakes.)

Bake 35 to 40 minutes or until center is set and edges puff and begin to crack. Cool in pan on wire rack. Refrigerate until chilled. Using foil as handles, lift from pan. Cut into bars.

"My mom sent me to the store with a food stamp

For a pack of cigarettes and a book at the newsstand (here)

Two dudes ran up, jumped out of a blue van

I looked down at the ground and picked up a huge branch

I swung it at the first dude, the other one with him

So, he tried to rush, I swept his legs pinned him and bit him

He came back with six or seven dudes screaming "Get Him!"

*~Eminem * 'Food Stamp'*

Detroit - Ten years earlier:

Kevin Woods saunters with effortless swag, quickly crisscrossing the potholes of Seven Mile, bobbing his starter row of mini-twists, hair in sync to Kanye West booming on his gigantic Sony headphones. Even though he's on foot he shines in his black Adidas hoodie, velvet sweats, a thick white gold chain with classic black and white shell toes. Kevin is in a zone rapping and air drumming along with Mr. West, "I feel the pressure, under more scrutiny, and what I do? Act more stupidly, bought more jewelry, more Louie V, my Mama couldn't get through to me..."

"Ayo K- Swizzle!" A familiar voice booms from down the street by the gun shop, it's his boy Zach walking towards him on the opposite side of the street with homie Quinton.

"Ayo homies!" Kevin yells back as Quinton gives him the finger salute, Kevin replies the same. They make motions to head towards each other.

"This dude..." Kevin snickers to himself watching Zach lose his sagging pants while attempting to cross the street.

A blue van encroaches behind the distracted Kevin as he watches Zach stumbling on his pants cuffs.

Kevin snickers "Ahh you can't even walk N..." The van startles him, cuts him off as two dudes jump out, start rushing towards him. "What the?" Disconcerted, Kevin backpedals and grabs a nearby tree branch, he swings at the first dude, then the second. Ducking and rolling the man springs back up and rushes again, Kevin swings at his legs, tripping him, and pinning him to the ground. Dude is still swinging as Kevin finds himself biting him to subdue him. The man screams as his boy pushes Kevin off.

"Yo Kev what the heck! Yo!" Quinton and Zach are rushing up as the unknown men scramble into the van. They are barely inside the van as the driver steps on the gas spurting up gravel to escape. Quinton exchanges a few blows with an attacker dangling outside the sliding van door before they bounce out into the street and get away.

"We'll be back Woods!" The man yells out as they disappear in traffic.

Quinton brushes himself off angrily as he scowls at the traffic, "For real yo, you know these fools? I'm gonna get my boy Jaquan and bust a cap in somebody!"

"Wasn't that kid in JV punching out grown men?"

"So, Kev, who the hell was that man? You in some type of trouble or something?" Zach huffs surveying the scene of the crime.

"No, no, I have no idea, seriously yo, that was some illness for real. All I know is Mama gave me the food stamp card to run to the corner store to get some milk, eggs, cheese and a crosswords puzzle book, man, then I saw you dudes and bam it was a wrap." Kevin pants out of breath.

"You really had no idea? Man, that didn't seem like a random jump nah mean. They knew your name."

"Ayo, his voice did sound familiar…" Kevin gasps, getting himself together.

"That's that bull man, I'm getting my homies, we taking these fools out!"

"Quinton chill, no need to escalate it man, we need to use some strategies and figure out things. Trust, I don't like this yo, I don't like this at all! Man, let me go get this crap." They head to the corner store as Kevin seeks out the requested items.

Quinton continues bouncing around full of hyped up energy, "And wait a minute, since when does the Woods family need food stamps anyway?"

"Since the auto plant shut down and everything around it, Zeke's business has been dry! Thought you knew!"

"Shut the front door, the Woods family are even feeling the effects of the Detroit shut down! I remember the heyday of Zeke's; bros were packed wall to wall waiting for that fried fish, collard greens, okra, chicken fried steak, pork ribs..."

"Black-eyed peas, cornbread, gizzards, ham hocks, sweet potatoes..."

"You two are bringing back serious memories. I miss those days; the restaurant is struggling. Dad is over Casstown right now having to pick up cheaper meat now!"

"Man, I'm getting hungry! What were those ones, Ox jaws or something?"

"Pigs feet" Quinton laughs, finally mellowing out.

"Yeech, I'm good on that and Chitterlings." Zach scrunches his nose.

"Cause you a redhead freckled face fool, you grew up on some escargot or something. Don't know nothin bout that down-home food." Quinton jabs Zach.

"The swine rejects is what Master fed the slaves, establishing a new tradition injected into our DNA." Quinton makes a face at the serious Kevin.

"Oh, hell no, isn't that snails or something?"

"You tell me!"

"Bro, I grew up on Ramen noodles, mayo sandwiches, and Kool-Aid just like ya'll. Trailer parks don't have any escargot or whatever the hell that is!"

Quinton continues, "Hmmm and that government cheese whew! Obama needs to bring back that service right to the house, the cheese, the bread, milk, eggs, and cereal. Loved getting those joint's right at the door!" He makes a motion opening a door then rubbing his stomach.

"Fool, cause you were too lazy to run to the corner store to buy it!" Kevin jabs him as they laugh.

"Hey though, that government cheese was the whip! Last forever, cut a bit of mold off, keep eating!" Zach injects.

"That doesn't even sound right, probably was some type of experiment on us, probably injected with pesticides or something. Gotta eat the right foods that Mother Nature intended for us, fresh, organic, from the earth, not all that preservatives, msg, and stuff you can't pronounce." Kevin gets serious on them.

"There you go with that conspiracy bull again Kevin, lighten up homie. Like they would do something like that to us!"

Kevin and Zach both stare at Quinton deadpan. He shrugs, "What?"

Tires squeal startling them as they exit the store, the van is back.

Kevin shakes his head, "Are you kidding me?"

Quinton moves towards the van fists up, "Bring it!"

The sliding door pops open and now six or seven guys leap out, "Get him!"

"Aw hell no!" Quinton backs into Kevin and Zach as the men rush them, they turn and run. Men race behind them as the van squeals tires and follow in pursuit. Quinton races behind a house, "Come on!"

The boys leap over a fence as sirens ring out in the neighborhood. Kevin's heart falls into his stomach as he hears a large commotion erupting from the next block. The small trio scramble through brush and backyards avoiding Seven Mile.

"Yo man, I'm pisst, just bought these K-Swiss," Quinton grumbles as they peer over another fence. "I'll just have to throw these out, grass stains are murderous."

"Seriously though? What size do you wear man? I'll take them!" Zach pleads thirstily.

Men are heard yelling as police arrive.

"Guys... back to the present? We have cops and unknown assailants battling it out and we don't know which way to go. Plus, I have damn eggs in my sack!" Kevin shakes his head.

Zach snickers, "Scrambled."

"Bruh, you have unknown assailants tracking you down like an Eminem song. Not us, you. We innocent accomplices. Dudes in a blue van, what the..." Zach pulls out a blunt listening to Quinton rattle on before pausing. "Bruh, did you really just pull out a blunt?"

"Dude, this was getting old, we just ran like a mile or something down Seven Mile. I got some type of sticky plant things on my socks, think I cut my leg, I'm tired, hungry, time for a smoke."

Quinton shakes his head before reaching out, "Bruh, don't be stingy."

"You two are unbelievable."

"Hey, what in Sam hill you boys doing on my lawn crushing my baby's flowers?" A booming voice rings out with the click of a gun.

"Let's go!"

****

Casstown - 10 years earlier.

Ezekiel Sr. is loading his van from the supply store, it's almost completely full as the sun is starting to set casting shadows. He's wedging a carton of flour into the cramped space when something scurrying about in the parking lot startles him. He looks around, shakes it off and keeps packing. It rolls underneath a car.

"What the? Who's there, what is that?"

He hears something like a child snickering. He looks under the cars, down the lot, doesn't see anything. He goes back to packing.

There is a laugh in the shadows. He looks around, "Who's there? Show yourself!" He grumbles and slams the door. "Damn kids."

He pulls out his keys when something flashes by the lone tree behind the lot. Squinting, he peers towards the tree as something seems to be standing beside it. It moves, laughs at him. It seems to be a little man, taunting, mocking him

"Who are you, what do you want?"

The little man stands a bit more erect, he seems to have horns and long fingernails. His little arm shakes, he rears a pointy nail towards Ezekiel. He speaks but is barely audible.

"Hey man, I don't know what you're on and I don't have any money, but I don't want any trouble. I'm going to go now." Ezekiel heads for his door when a huge rock suddenly dents his door. He wheels around at the little imp, he seems bigger. "Hey, what's the deal man? Who's going to pay for that?"

"Loser" The imp mutters.

"What you call me?"

"Loser!" He throws another rock bashing through the window of the van.

"Damn it!" Ezekiel slings a rock back as the imp laughs, his eyes glow. Ezekiel ends up throwing his keys.

"Dad!" Ezekiel almost swings on Kevin.

"Kevin, what, what the heck, don't do that. Where did you come from? Why are you here?"

"Mr. Woods, they after us, I don't know what's happening, we..." Zach pants, gasps.

"Slow down son, what is happening?"

"Dad, I don't know who they are, but somebody came at us. They called me out, tried to rush me, came twice. The second time they came back with more people."

"Wait, son, who is they? What did you do?"

"Nothing, I don't know dad. Think it has something to do with the restaurant, seriously."

Ezekiel looks at him curiously, remembers his keys and the encounter. Looks back towards the back of the lot.

"Mr. Woods, what's wrong, what are you looking at?" Quinton asks.

"I don't know, it's not there now. I need to find my keys, help me find them and I'll take you boys home and figure this out. Is that eggs running out of that bag?"

Kevin hides the ravaged bag behind him, "Dad, what happened to your window? Seriously, do we have the insurance for that?"

"Long story. Let's get the hell out of here. Come on guys." They start to head towards the back of the lot. Tires squeal and they turn to face a vehicles' blinding lights. It's the blue van. The doors open as they stand behind Ezekiel Sr.

"Well, well, the Woods clan and esteemed guests. Glad we can gather everybody together in this fine location in Casstown."

"Lyam Winkelman, my goodness, what do you want?" Ezekiel groans.

"That Lydell's dad?" Kevin whispers to his dad, Ezekiel nods and gives him the hand.

"Big Zeke, got your little man with you. Where's that punk little Zeke? You know the Woods clan owes me huge for what he did."

"Listen Lyam you are a conniving fool, think you Detroit's Donald Trump! The low rent version! Drop it, you have no evidence. This is ridiculous! We owe you nothing!"

"Dad, what, what is he talking about?"

"Oh, you don't know, *Uncle* Kevin?" Lyam snickers.

"Lyam, drop it. Listen, you and I know each other from the ol' Ford assembly lines, working side by side, day in and day out. We were on the same picket lines, working with the unions. Our children grew up together. Bro, we were family man. Why are you doing this?"

Lyam steps forward, along with Lydell and two other men flanking him. Another truck full of men are behind them. Lyam coughs up phlegm, covers his mouth with a handkerchief. He spits on the ground. Lydell whispers in his ear and Lyam shakes his head, "Screw that man, those assembly lines jacked my lungs up good. Listen Woods, $50k or everybody knows the foulness of your promising scholar discretion. We're going to be back every damn day causing havoc on everybody in your family until you pay. Zeke's Kitchen is done. I *own* it now."

"Dad, what is he talking about?" Kevin jerks forward, Lyam's men get in front. Quinton and Zach push forward, hyped up nervously.

"Boys calm down, we're not adding to Detroit's violence tonight. Mr. Winkelman and I will get this matter taken care of like gentlemen."

"We'll handle it by the Woods clan paying for Jr. sowing his seeds in my niece and running like a bitch damn it!"

"Sow his seed? Dad? What is he insinuating?"

"Ohh Lil Zeke got a kid?" Zach blurts out. Quinton jabs him in the gut.

"Not valid Zachary, he's talking out the side of his neck. Lyam lies..."

Lydell has to practically hold his father back "Truth big Zeke! You ignore the truth! You..."

"I don't want to hear this crap Lyam, boys let's go!"

Ezekiel attempts to get the boys towards the work van. Lyam coughs and spits, "Fact is you ignored your boy, he was jealous of his own flesh and blood sister Maureen who was in love with my niece Ria! You didn't approve, he didn't approve! That's not for the Woods men to decide now is it? He planned it out, got the girls drunk, once Mo was passed out he gave Ria the business! Took her virginity Zeke! Took her virginity!" Lyam is hoarse, yelling.

Kevin spots his father's eyes tearing up, unsure what to say or do to help. They are all in a state of confusion as the elder Winkelman has dropped a megaton bomb on them. Ezekiel leans against the van, gasping for air. Kevin goes to his aid, "Dad, what's wrong?"

"Yo, this is jacked up Kev." Quinton is gripping his fists. He pulls Zach with him towards the men who gang up pushing them backwards.

"Took her virginity Zekey! You hear me? That lovechild is on your hands' sir! Your responsibility and I'm here to make you pay! I bet that bottle of Scotch was yours too. The great Ezekiel Woods Sr. about to fold!"

Zach pulls the hesitant Quinton backwards, "Yo kid, not liking these odds."

"Yah punk ass Lydell, you couldn't handle me one on one, bring it!" Quinton talks smack as the men snicker at him.

Ezekiel is half crying, gasping for air as Kevin comforts him clumsily. He looks towards his son, "Your brother is a good boy, he made a mistake. He knows it's never right to take advantage of a woman, never son. He's been paying for it ever since, why he got into law. To make a difference, help people. He's just getting started, he should not have to pay like this. All of you have been the best, why I worked so hard." Kevin takes his hand and he squeezes it.

"You can sugar coat it all you want Zeke, that's considered date rape and you didn't handle it!" Lyam is bellowing over the boys, getting more hyped up.

"Date rape? Didn't some model accuse the Cos of that? That didn't go anywhere. He got away with it, lil Zeke can." Zach quips.

Everyone goes silent and looks at him in shock and dismay.

"Um, no?"

Kevin hits his friend in the jaw himself. "Damn Kev! What the hell?"

"See Zekey! Your own child is disgusted! Face the facts old man, your offspring, your pride and joy buried you! You're finished! Your restaurant is done! I own you! Mark my words!"

"I don't like them disrespecting you, Mr. Woods! Got me messed up!" Quinton pushes back between the men; the taller man punches him hard in the stomach. Quinton groans and doubles over. Gathering his strength Quinton punches at the man. Lydell punches at Kevin who punches back. Zach double-teams Lydell pushing him as a fight ensues.

"Boys! Boys! Stop it! Stop it!" The elder Woods crackles trying to step forward weakly to them.

Lyam grins wide watching the quarrel ensue, laughing. Sirens are heard in the background.

Zach hits the ground with a swollen lip. Quinton is on the pavement still swinging while getting kicked at by several men.

Kevin steps back from the melee, Ezekiel grabs his arm. "No son...not your fight." He looks past Kevin, towards the lone tree at the back of the lot, his eyes go wide, like he sees a ghost.

"Dad, dad! What are you looking at?" Kevin attempts to hold his father up who slumps against the van, his face frozen.

"The Nain Rouge...Nain Rouge." He mutters barely audible. His skin goes a lighter shade of brown. His fist clutching his chest.

"What? What?"

Ezekiel looks up towards his son and mouths out "I Love you", before slumping behind the vehicle.

"Dad! No no!" His father is unresponsive.

Lyam snaps his fingers as his cronies' stop, "Time to move boys. He gets what he deserves."

"What the hell?" Quinton gets off the ground and stumbles back to them.

"Someone call 911! Call 911! Dad! Dad!" Kevin shakes his father.

Lyam snickers, motions for his son and men to leave. "Will see you in hell Big Zeke!" He cackles as he slams the vehicles door.

"Hey Kev, I'll be back to holla at you and lil Zeke." Lydell winks at them before they start their van and hightail it out of there before Detroit police arrive.

Kevin sobs on his lifeless father as Quinton punches the side of the van. Zach looks in shock nursing his lip, "Hey any of you hear still hear someone laughing? Man, that's jacked up."

Police and an ambulance arrive while the boys watch over the lifeless Ezekiel Woods Sr.

"Listen to the rhyme, it's a black date fact

Percentile rate of date rape is fat

This is all true to the reason of the skeezing

You got the right picking but you're in the wrong season

If you're in the wrong season, that means you gotta break

Especially if a squad tries to cry out rape"

*~The Infamous Date Rape * A Tribe Called Quest*

Present day:

Kwame aka Kevin Woods sobs as he holds his mother's hand in the hospital bed. The only sounds are the quiet hum of the equipment keeping her alive. Holding her hand tightly he chokes on his emotions, “Selfishness’ comes in many forms, mine is gigantic.”

Eat @Zeke's Part XII:

Tart Cherry Pie

Tart Cherry Cobbler

5 (14.5 ounce) cans tart pitted cherries packed in water, drained
1 cup brown sugar
1/2 cup white sugar
3 tablespoons quick-cooking tapioca
1/2 teaspoon almond extract
1/4 teaspoon cinnamon
1 pinch salt
1 tablespoon butter, diced
1 recipe pastry for double-crust pie
2 tablespoons milk

Preheat oven to 400 degrees F (200 degrees C). In a large bowl, gently stir the cherries, brown sugar, and white sugar until all the sugar has dissolved. Mix in the tapioca, almond extract, cinnamon, and salt. Let stand 15 minutes. Pour into a 9x13 inch baking dish, and dot with butter. Roll pie pastry into a rectangle slightly larger than the baking dish, and place over the cherries. Tuck in corners, and make several slits in the dough. Brush with milk. Bake 45 minutes in the preheated oven, until crust is lightly browned and filling is bubbly. Cool 1 hour before serving.

Two sides to every story

One man's gloom is another man's glory

Sun to a shadow, rose to a thorn

There ain't no fury like a woman scorned

Prince - "Fury"

Detroit

Mama was awake.

The skies over Detroit were ominously purple as clouds that gurgled and rumbled threatened a downpour but never produced any water. A single drop splashes off of Mama's hospital window and dislodges a nearby leaf off of a White Birch. The leaf floats between the clouds and random drips. From the underside of the leaf, a worm appears scrambling to stay afloat. A dove appears, snatches up the leaf and worm.

Rummaging through the ruins of Zeke's Kitchen, Silvia looks in awe as the kitchen portion still stands. The up to date appliances and equipment her father worked so hard to install were barely touched by the fire. As for the rest, nothing but charred remains of ash and mud. Was completely surreal.

Freddy, Pook, Tyrone, Akee, and Bama walk through the rubble sifting through the ash. Their friend John George from Detroit Blight Busters arrives with a large squad of volunteers armed with tools to help clean the site. Freddy waves them over. "So sorry for your loss my friend." John reaches out to Freddy as they lock shoulders and pat each other back. John looks over to the Woods sisters.

Maureen pulls out a picture of her father and civil rights protesters and cries. Akee approaches and pats her back, "Miss Woods, so sorry I am." Maureen sobs gripping his elbow. Nods as he consoles her, wiping away her tears.

In her half-closed eyes, she blinks, looks above her, squints. The majestic dove is circling above them, soaring gracefully, symbolic. She locks eyes with Silvia who spots the bird also. They have a moment as the clouds open up, the sun shines through these ominous purple clouds.

Maureen screams as the bird coos and craps in her eye. She shrieks. Akee has to help her keep her footing as she full-fledged freaks out, shaking her hands, swatting her face. The men start snickering before laughing hysterically.

Silvia tilts her head sideways, "What the heck?" Her cell is buzzing incessantly. She fumbles for it in the mayhem of her sister freaking out.

"Help me! Somebody get hot water and soap! Get me some vinegar! Medic! Doctor! Somebody!"

Silvia reads the text as she takes a moment to comprehend, she gasps, checks the voicemail, screams.

"What the Sam hill now?" Pook groans

"Mama is awake! Mama is awake!! Seriously? Stop messing around Mo! Let's go!!"

"Mama? What the what! I call shotgun!" Tyrone yells.

"Lord have mercy, oh happy day. I'll get my car also, some of you can ride with me." Freddy starts sauntering towards the street.

Pook laughs, "I'm good, that ol' '86 Continental with no shocks, dang death trap. I'll ride with Silvia."

"Guys, it says she's cooking for everyone? Um, we gotta go."

"Cooking? I can finally get my eggs and bacon! Whoo hoo!" Tyrone does a gig.

"Serious? Lord Jesus, what is your mother up too now? We need to go! Can you keep up with me in that eco-boost thing?"

Silvia snickers "We'll see, let's hope your back shocks don't give out and you disappear into a pothole." Pook gives her a one finger salute.

Maureen is on her knees trying to get to Silvia's car, "My eye, my eye, I can't see, I can't see. Wait, wait!"

Silvia huffs, her usually glamorous sister was doing too much, taking this bird poo to the extreme. Reluctantly she gets out to help her. She pauses, looking up at the circling birds and vibrant colored clouds. She pondered, this day seemed quite ominous with just a sprinkle of hope, and it was quite off catching. She lets out a heavy sigh to help her traumatized sister into her car.

Elsewhere in Detroit

Ezekiel sits in his BMW outside of his office, dribbles of rain blur his image inside. He wipes his brow, deep in concentration. For once, he is unsure of himself.

His cell buzzes incessantly, he picks it up, stares at it a moment contemplating, ends up throwing it to the side. Gathering his courage he picks up his briefcase and exits the vehicle, pausing to gaze directly into the drizzling rain before heading into the office.

The lights are dim as the business is only working with a skeleton crew. His partners Marty and Theodore Simon are in the meeting room along with their accountant Aspen Jobson.

"Ez E is finally in the house, come in my boy and let's celebrate!" Marty is red nose busted already pouring some Vodka at the private bar. "Shots, shots, shots!" Theodore and Aspen shake their head. Ezekiel rolls his eyes, sighs, walks over and takes the glass.

"You're late Woods, don't even know how you made partner with all of your trivial indiscretions distracting you. Can we get this show on the road finally?" Theodore grumbles.

"Good to see you too Theo" Ezekiel snickers.

Aspen casually walks over to him hands him a folder of documents. He looks over her long legs accented by her five-inch heels. She follows his gaze and shakes her head. "Please look over your documents, if everything is in order, you can sign over your portion of the insurance policies and the deeds."

"Everybody else will fall in line, not like anything is left. Amazing coincidence don't you think?" Theodore quips. Ezekiel huffs and looks begrudgingly over the papers.

"Ezekiel my boy, don't sweat it. Your father would have been okay with this, every story has an ending and he would have understood the time has come. Change is always for certain."

"Not like this, something doesn't feel right."

"Really get cold feet Jr? You were the one that even suggested we go this route. You wanted to better the community, improve the neighborhood, and make it better than when you were a kid. How ironic indeed, all that talk was about nothing." Theodore huffs.

Marty pours another drink, "Zeke, listen, gentrification doesn't necessarily have to be a dirty word! We'll broker new condos and parks and white boys with dreadlocks riding bicycles in no time!" He takes a shot and burps, follows with a chaser.

"And don't forget this carries a 1.2 million dollar purse for brokering this deal, Mr. Woods," Aspen adds in not even looking up from her calculations.

Theodore lights a cigar, "You know lil Zeke, piecing together all of these parcels gives us a demanding portion on the east side. Redeveloping this is not only smart for us, it's definitely smart for Detroit!"

"It doesn't feel right shutting out the very folks who built this city and stayed strong. This has morphed into something not recognizable. You tell me there is someone else besides that snake Winkleman? I don't want to see him anywhere around this project. Makes me want to puke in my mouth. Who is this other so-called mystery partner pushing this?"

He checks his messages. "Well well, looks like our primary funder, aka this so-called mystery partner wants to join the party and meet everyone. Right on time. He's here."

"Really? This should be interesting. I have low faith in you guys after that rat's appearance. Really like to see which devil I'm dancing with."

Ezekiel reads over the contract as an entourage enters. He is caught up dissecting it when he notices the decorated distinct cane rapping on the linoleum. He looks up making eye contact with the smirking Lydell Winkelman himself. Ezekiel leans back, he feels his stomach flip, this isn't right.

"Ezekiel my boy, so good to see you. The rat is back! Glad we're finally doing business together. Is about time."

"I told you idiots not to bring this dog back here! Excuse my candor, but Simon brothers this that bull..."

"Ezekiel, my ol' friend, you set this in motion yourself so many years ago. This is the direct results of your illicit transgressions. Against my family, me keeping your dirty little secrets. Should have envisioned your eventual payback. I gave you ample opportunity to make amends - and you failed to do so." Winkelman quips smugly.

Ezekiel stands, brushes the papers off the desk. The lawyers look at him in confusion. Lydell smirks at him, stands his ground as they glare at each other.

"Mr. Woods, Mr. Winkelman is correct in the regards you did set this in motion, drew up the plans, and even suggested the location..."

Ezekiel cuts off Aspen, "And my initial plan was not a total gentrification of my old neighborhood! These current plans will destroy the neighborhood! That was NOT the plan! Especially not with this demon!"

Aspen sucks her lips and sits back glaring over at Theodore. He starts to react but his brother interrupts.

"Like I said, my friend! We needed a partner and Lye came through with ample funds! Gentrification doesn't have to be a bad word I say again! Everything is coming into place Ezekiel, roll with it!" Marty laughs and takes a shot.

"Not acceptable! I am not signing a deal with the devil! You guys purposely withheld this information. You know that's grounds for a lawsuit right? I am about to sue all of you, take this whole firm and have all of you backstabbers work for me afterward."

"The devil comes in different forms doesn't it little Zeke? You like to dance." Lydell leans in.

"Lydell, don't play with me!"

"Ezekiel cut the crap! You know you did it!" Marty guffaws spilling alcohol. Ezekiel looks at him surprised before he makes eyes with the smirking Lydell.

"Ah contrary, information was shared with you via your partner which is very legal. As far as we know you were aware of everyone's involvement with this project. We all have had access to the same information." Theodore looks deadpan at Ezekiel.

"Partner? Which partner shared this with me? This is ridiculous. I don't have to stand for this, see you guys in court and I can erase the Simon name from the title!" Ezekiel is slamming stuff into his attaché. The door slams.

Lydell looks down the hallway, "Well well, looks like your silent partner is here. This is the real surprise! She-devil incarnate! Amazing you didn't see this coming."

"Looks like we have another surprise guest."

Ezekiel frowns, "Excuse me?" He looks around the corner, his mouth opens in shock, instant sweat on his face. He wipes his face and stands up straight, very discombobulated.

"What's the matter hubby? Looks like you've seen a ghost." Kayla stands above him, dressed sharply in a suit, heels, and her hair done. She has herself together.

She smiles before sitting down near Lydell who attempts to touch her shoulder and she moves away. He grimaces.

"What? Seriously? This is my so-called partner? Don't make me laugh! This has to be a joke, what grounds do you have to pull this coup?"

"Coup? I guess that is a fancy name for this takeover, *honey*. For better or for worse right? Deceitful whore of a husband. I didn't even do crap to you to deserve this. Yet you kept me hocked up on those magic lil blue pills, and booze and wine all while you did me wrong messing around with your slutty secretary and Lord knows what else..."

"Excuse me, as I laugh! I don't think so! Complete ridiculousness! From the crazed woman who bashed into this very building mind you. There is a reason for those pills you think? You morons want to flirt with disaster? What type of businessmen are you? You don't prove anything..."

"I'm sorry Zekey. I had no choice. They asked, and I talked." Ms. Kane appears from nowhere, her eyes moist. Ezekiel wipes his sweaty brow. The walls were closing in.

"Shut it pinhead, *your lies* are the complete ridiculousness! I'm tired of hearing your bloated ego-maniacal narcissistic drivel, go cry me a river Lil Zekey, lil

Zeke is about right. Tiny boy! Your father had class, you are a monster." Kayla injects.

"How dare you! Am I a monster? You really think you have me backed into a corner? All of you! This... this evil person. Kayla, you coming in here with crooked Lydell of all people! Do you realize the root word of his very name? LIE - dell - seriously?"

"Excuse me?" Lydell arches his eyebrow.

Kayla slaps Marty's glass out of his hand smashing it to the floor, "I'm stopping this ranting right now! Crap didn't start here with this whore!" Ms. Kane's mouth drops. The drunken Marty takes the bottle.

"What? What now? What other damn surprises could this awful night bring about? Tell me dear wifey, what did all this start with, what? Spit it out!" His own words frothing from his mouth.

Kayla stands, glares at him "Two words my dear hubby, Ria Vergeman." Ezekiel stops in his tracks, his jaw drops in shock. He sits down with a hard thud.

"You've been a naughty, naughty boy a long-time you idiot. To think I thought I had a decent man. Think I wouldn't have found out? Paybacks a mutha now isn't it *husband*. Now I have to provide papers." Everybody quietly looks in suspense as she produces packets. "One; paternity results. Two; non-disclosure documents. You may find the details of the evidence you left behind, nice and frozen here. Three; divorce papers. Wife is entitled to half."

She slaps them on his lap as Ezekiel for once is speechless. "You enjoy chess so much, my dear husband. Checkmate".

The room is quiet as Kayla relishes in finally having her day above her husband. As he looks aghast over the papers a single tear splats on the paper. He lifts his head in shame looking into her glassy eyes before she wipes her face. Her trembling hands' yanks off her wedding ring and throws it on the floor by his feet as he looks dumbfounded. They stare at each other for several moments.

She extends a long fingernail as he follows her reach, she taps his Shinola watch. Tap, tap taps. Clearing her throat, she softly speaks, "By the way, your mother is awake, about an hour ago. She asked about you. She's cooking, ironically. Your mother, she's a rock. I'm elated my children have her at least. Oh yeah, she mentioned somebody named Kwame is there. Might want to go."

She continues tapping hard at the watch, Ezekiel is oblivious, and it starts to crack. Marty gasps and belches, "That's Detroit's finest Shinola! Don't do it Kay!"

She rethinks the watch. "I did buy that for him. I used to be somebody. I will again." She reveals a wrapped tart cherry pie from her purse and pushes it at his trembling hands. She smiles.

Ezekiel is beside himself, "What foolishness is this..."

"A grand symbol of your foolishness! Now go to your mother you idiot. I'll be waiting for my signatures." Kayla puts herself together. She gathers her purse and heads for the exit.

Ezekiel snaps out of it, stammers, "KAYLA! Wait, this isn't over! Where are you going?"

"Don't worry where I'm going. You need to get to your mother."

She pauses by the construction area fixing the hole she made. She smirks at it before strolling out of the office quietly. Lydell gets up chuckling, he slaps Ezekiel on his back as his menacing laugh gets louder. He snaps his fingers as his entourage follows. Lydell drops his handkerchief in disrespect before leading his cronies out.

Kayla's car turns on outside, Ezekiel awakens, shakes, "KAYLA! Come back! This isn't over! Damn it! KAYLA!" Weakened, he crumbles into the chair as his partners watch in silence.

"Well, that was enough entertainment for tonight, it was great doing business with you my friend. Change is immanent for our partnership. We'll address that after we square this away. Godspeed." Theodore disappears into the private office bathroom suite.

"We will expect these signed papers in the morning, Mr. Woods." Aspen re-positions the documents on the table and exits.

Sobbing, Ms. Kane looks longingly at the crushed man before disappearing into the shadows.

Marty is passed out drunk, mouth wide, snoring. His drink spills onto the linoleum.

Ezekiel quivers, yells "KAYLAAAAAAAA!!!" Repeats.

Eat@Zeke's:

Part XIII

Mama's Potluck (Epilogue)

Creamed Corn

18 medium ears corn, shucked
3 tablespoons unsalted butter, plus more for serving
3/4 cup chopped yellow onion
1 1/2 teaspoons kosher salt, divided
1/4 cup heavy whipping cream
1 tablespoon chopped fresh thyme
1/4 teaspoon ground black pepper
1/8 teaspoon ground red pepper

Holding a long, sharp knife at a downward angle, cut tips from corn kernels (about 4 cups). Stand each cob over a large bowl. Using the back of a spoon, scrape downward to remove pulp (about 3 cups). In a 10-inch skillet, melt butter over medium heat. Add onion; cover and cook over medium-low heat until softened, about 15 minutes.

Add corn kernel tips, pulp, and 1 teaspoon salt; bring to a boil over medium-high heat. Cover, reduce heat, and simmer until corn is tender, about 35 minutes, stirring occasionally. Uncover; stir in cream, thyme, black pepper, red pepper, and remaining 1/2 teaspoon salt. Cook until thickened, 8 to 10 minutes. Serve with extra butter.

Detroit

Beads of sweat form on Ezekiel's Woods forehead as he looks up at the hot spring sun in Detroit. Rain clouds are dissipating as beams of light swoop over drenched land illuminating even the darkest corners. He wipes his brow and licks his parched lips.

Squinting, he tries to make out somebody in the distance coming towards him. He rubs his eyes as his vision is blurred. Shapes and people morph together into unknown shapes. Sounds come across like a warped record played backward. Ezekiel swallows hard, he didn't know whether he was having an adverse reaction to medication or having a hard attack. A ghostly woman floats towards him speaking gibberish.

He shudders his head in bewilderment, "Kayla?"

The woman speaks louder gibberish while shaking her fist.

"I don't know, I simply don't know!" He responds in frustration. He has no clue.

Randomly the woman comes into focus, "Hey stupid! Get out of the retention basin! What drugs are you on? I'm getting security ya moron!" The gardener puts down her electric saw before retrieving her mobile.

Bewildered, Ezekiel roils his head. Where was he? He notices pedestrians stopping to look at him, point, take pictures. He feels soaked. He looks down. He is waist deep in the hospital retention basin.

Panicking, he pivots in retreat, his attaché case flips open, precious papers fly into the water adding misery to humiliation. Suddenly his watch alarm erupts, he looks at it against the beaming sun. Its face crackled veins from Kayla's angst the night before. It's time.

Hospital

Sinking down under the water, slipping down under

Drifting out into the water, missing down under

Sinking down under the water, slipping down under

Drifting out into the water, missing down under

Have mercy, have mercy, have mercy, have mercy

Have mercy on us all (Repeat)

~Have Mercy - "Eryn Allen Kane"

Fourth-floor Hospital

The hospital cafeteria is unusually packed on the weekday afternoon. Crisp shafts of light shine through the large windows casting long shadows across the room. Its standing room only. The Vergeman sisters are chatting it up with nurses near the soda pop machines. Tyrone is deeply emotional with his plate of deep fried fish, macaroni, and cheese, okra, potatoes, and gravy. Taking each bite with such an emotional transgression that his mind shuts down while his soul is lifted to higher elevations.

Ackee and Bama are talking politics with Pastor Ceopha Clements. Pook leads his kitchen team staff of Sugar, Tanya, and Moco, serving trays of steaming hot food to the packed room full of Zeke's Kitchen fans and hospital staff. Dr. Sharon is conversing with Kylie about what it means to be a doctor as Kevin Jr. is getting to know Matador and Milo running among the crowd.

"Hi Daddy!" His son hugs him as Matador seems to be the only one happy to see him as Kylie looks away from her father.

A wisp of blonde hair, Sasha, pops out of the crowd and scrunches her nose. She elbows her bestie Utopia who looks up at the disgraced Ezekiel with contempt. He feels her accusatory stare sear through him as she sits between Sasha and an Indian woman he later discovers is his nephew's mother Ponyi. Quinton, Zach, and Jaquan are all chopping it up deep in a conversation about the Pistons and Cavaliers. They drop quiet seeing Ezekiel.

Big Moe stands up, towering over him, sullenly shaking his head. “Mr. Woods, all due respect, your disgusting inflated ego needs a heterogeneous turbulence to rattle you to your core." Ezekiel looks up at the angry giant and loosens up his collar.

The room drops to a whisper as he approaches the front. A dreaded man hangs close to his mother who seems oblivious to all the tension. She is in her own little world jolly, giggling like a schoolgirl between this man and Freddy Styles enveloping her with attention. Freddy gives him a confident wink that disturbs him to his core. He and his mother are in their seventies, but the obvious flirtation still bothers him. Heck, this is his mother.

Hearing a tapping noise on the floor he knows immediately baby sis Mo is on his left tapping on her high heel. He glances over. Her face is puffy, eyes narrowed at him. Her wife, Bailey, is holding her hand, showing support. "Mo", he chokes a bit.

"Ezekiel", she growls.

Silvia arrives with drinks, sharing them with her mother, Freddy and this dreaded man. She smiles at him "Hey man, bout time you arrived! Where's Kayla?"

"Sis", Mo hisses.

"What? What? What did I miss?" Silvia asks innocently.

"Son! Come here!" Mama notices him. He goes and hugs her hard. "I love you son."

"Mama, don't scare us like that. Are you okay?" He's fighting back tears.

"No, but everything will be okay."

"Why are you cooking today? You need to be resting." He keeps wondering why this dreaded man is rubbing her shoulders and Silvia is fawning all over him.

"Son, you do your lawyering. I cook. It's who I am and I'm proud of it. Everybody here can attest to that!" The room claps in response. She continues "Be proud of what you do, and you'll make it right" She looks deep into his eyes. He gulps, loosens his collar more, she must have heard of his blunders, crap.

"I love you mother, so much." He hugs her hard tearing up.

"I love you too son, so happy to have you both here with me. I feel complete."

His mother clasped his ears, a throwback to what she used to do when he was a boy, choking him up. This was getting very uncomfortable. This dreaded man was looking at him and grinning. He was ready to pounce.

"Do you have a problem man?"

He claps, "Never ever seen the mighty Ezekiel flustered, was worth coming for this!" The dreaded man snickers.

Ezekiel almost passes out, he can recognize his brother's voice anywhere. "Wait, what? You just said both here? Kevin?" He looks at him in utter amazement.

"Seriously? Was this too much for your brother? And by the way, it's Kwame brother, Kwame!" He points to his Jamaican style and laughs.

"Yes, I, I...!" Ezekiel stutters, dumbfounded. Kwame laughs and reaches out for his brother. Ezekiel blinks in shock before finally submitting and hugging him. The watching, eerily quiet room erupts in applause.

"About time!" Silvia joins in the embrace tearing up. Mama looks on satisfied.

"I'm sorry bro, really I am." Ezekiel musters.

"It's all love here brother."

A hard fingernail jabs him in his side. Ezekiel turns around and gets a slap on his face. Flabbergasted, he expects to see Kayla.

"Maureen Patricia Woods!" Mama gasps.

Ezekiel winces before eyeing Maureen glaring at him. "Glad you two found some bro love during Mama's comeback and all, but you still have some unfinished business here."

Kwame grabs his shoulder, "Hey bro, you might want to listen. Fam just filled me in. It's been a minute. Feels insane now. I'm glad it's being cleared."

Ezekiel winces, a drop of sweat pouring off his forehead. His confusion clouding his brain. He is rattled. "Mo, how dare you! I know we have our diff..."

"Shut it Lil Zeke! Let me finish!"

"Mo! Now is not the time to iron this..."

"Hey! Let her speak jerk or I'll lay your boogie ass to sleep." Bailey springs into action, fist raised, ready to protect her girl."

"Oh miss, let me put your lil' dyke..."

"Ezekiel Quinzell Woods! Let your sister speak! It's now that time son, let's bury this!" Mama practically stands up as Kwame and Freddy assist her to sit back down. Dr. Sharon rushes over to check her vitals. Mama's watery eyes speak to him as he realizes he's in the wrong. "Your father would be very ashamed of you right now Zekey. You need to make things right, starting with that lil girl right there."

"Wait, what? Mo and I been beefing since we were kids, about that time she was discovering herself. Why is it now we need to clear this when we should be honoring your comeback, I don't understand? This is nonsense."

"NO! This is not nonsense! You violated that little girl, Ezekiel. Do you not understand the heartbreak you've caused? With all your success and accomplishments, my wonderful grandchildren. We couldn't be prouder of you. But with this issue son, I need to see this resolved before..." She pauses as the room goes quiet. She continues with a whisper, "We raised you better than that, you are supposed to be my shining star, how could you?"

"Mama, what are you talking about?" The desperation in his voice is enhanced by the circle around him growing smaller. Ezekiel looks nervously about the enclosed space with Moe, Jaquan, Pook, Moco, Sugar, Ackee, Zach, Tawnya, Tyrone, Bama all breathing down his neck, seemingly ready to attack. The elder Vergemen Sisters are practically seething. Pastor Ceopha and Preacher Man merely open their Bibles to pray! Ezekiel gulps, peering through the mob he sees Ponyi usher out his Matador with Milo and Kevin Jr.

"Son... you need to make things right. This lil' girl needs her father."

Ezekiel looks over at his mother, perplexed. Maureen sobs in front of him as Bailey holds her. Ezekiel realizes this wasn't just about her.

"I, I don't understand..."

Something draws him to Kylie, she rocks her head no. Why is she glaring at him so hard? Her eyes plead with him as he follows her arm, she is squeezing Utopia's hand tightly. He tries to comprehend why his babysitter is glaring at him with such passion, he looks into Utopia's eyes confused. She has been crying. Sasha is by her side holding her other hand, eyes narrowed at him. Sasha pulls a faded Polaroid picture out of her purse and passes it to Utopia. Utopia rubs the picture carefully and then holds it up for him to see. It's Ria Vergeman.

"Son...you need to make things right" Mama whispers into his soul.

Utopia puts the picture in his shaking hand. She wipes away tears. "You remember her, don't you? My mother."

Ezekiel mouths out "Your mother?"

Her eyes moist they confirm yes in response. Everything suddenly makes sense. He clasps his hand over his mouth. A tear develops on his face.

"And you're saying that, that..." He can't even say it. Instinctively he glances over at Dr. Sharon who shakes her head that it was true.

"Trust, we had a sample, jerk." Sasha sneers as Utopia elbows her. "What?"

Maureen jabs him again, "Yes Zekey poo, your pee pee made a baby!" She pulls out papers of official results and pushes them at his chest. "Yes, wifey knew, she's the one copped your DNA. Why you think she don't like your trifling ass? Got this, legal and quickly. So, yes you moron, she's your child my dear *brother*! The direct consequences of your idiotic actions! Why you think I never forgave you, duh! Why do you think Kevin…Oops Kwame, my bad, had to run? Get over yourself! Do something, dang. That's what I'm talking about." She pushes him as he stumbles forward, weakly.

Bailey holds her, calming her. "I think by George he's getting it baby."

The surrounding circle of people seems to merge into a blurry glob. The air about him is stifled as anxiety snakes up his body. He feels faint, things are going black. He steps back woozy. A voice stands out.

"Dad, make it right like G Mama said." Kylie's whisper breaks through the darkness as she reaches out and grips his hand. He looks into her pleading eyes, tears streaming down her cheeks. He looks to his equally crying mother. You could hear somebody swallow.

Ezekiel exhales, defeated, accepting. "I, I, I'm so sorry. I didn't know. I didn't know. I... Please, I beg for your forgiveness. All of you." Trembling, he takes Utopia's hands. She breaks out crying and they embrace. He hugs her tightly as the group erupts in applause, Kylie joins their embrace. "I didn't know... I didn't know..."

He reaches out to Maureen who hesitates, shaking her head no. Mama and Bailey prod her before she joins the family hug. Everybody is crying.

Joyous, Mama beams behind the jovial room, "Thank you God for my family."

Ezekiel sobs, "I will make it right for you Utopia. Kev…I mean Kwame. Vergeman's..." The Vergemen sisters suck their lips, nod in approval.

In the corner of the room, a silent observer watches over the reunion. He smiles and shakes his head satisfied. He looks over at the lil' imp in the opposite corner. Ezekiel Sr. waves his finger no, sending the disgruntled Nain Rouge on his way.

The children start arriving back into the room, the next generation of Woods spot their grandfather. He waves at them, then nods to his beloved wife. She blows him a kiss. His smile is wide as the children smile back and wave before he slowly disappears in the darkness of the corner.

SIX MONTHS LATER - ARTIST VILLAGE - DETROIT

The crowd is long and deep outside and inside the colorful Artist Village on Lahser Street. Neo-soul and funk wafts over the eager crowd lined up to see the event.

Silvia and Maureen along with their extended family help Java House owner Alicia serve up coffee, tea, and goodies to patrons filtering in. Freddy Style's hawks 'Save Zeke's Kitchen' and 'Occupy Zeke's' t-shirts for sale to help bring back the restaurant. Monique Porter, from Sirna Tea, demonstrates healthy nutritional eating and drinking expertise with samples from her unique brand for the diverse urban culture. Pleze Moore from Detroit's Related Filmworks is busy shooting video of the celebration. Team members from the Lions, Pistons, Tigers and the Red Wings make guest appearances. One of the premiere Detroit artists Chazz Miller does drawings on the spot for concertgoers.

Kwame drops the beat on his drums as his band the Kommandoz light up the center stage in the open Artist Village area. A nice line up of Detroit artists such as Royce da 5'9, Dwele, Kem, Black Milk and Oddisee line up the night along with Motown Vets like Aretha and Smokey, all in support of Zeke's and the non-profit Blight Busters. Rumor has even Eminem was in attendance. LoVision offers music education to a handful of challenged children in attendance. The operator of the venue and Blight Busters John George, greets everyone shaking their hands in appreciation of their support. John and the Woods go way back. Blight Busters plan to help Styles community center clean up the rest of Zeke's debris and surrounding blight.

During the celebration Utopia, Kylie, Matador, Kevin Jr. and Sasha along with their family and friends dance in the center section. Lights and people surround them, cheering them on. Utopia looks to the stage where their dad has dusted off his old saxophone and joins his brother's group to jam. He looks back at them and smiles.

The Woods are front and center as Silvia and Maureen join their brothers on stage and link arms together. They are joined by Freddy, The Vergeman sisters, Tyrone, Bailey, Akee, Quinton, Tyrone, Zach, Moe, Jacquan and his little brother Jory, Pook, Ponyi, Tanya, Moco, Carlton, even Adanna, and the Preacher Man wearing 'Occupy Zeke's' shirts complete with Flapjack Jesus. The supportive crowd erupts in chants; "Eat at Zeke's! Eat at Zeke's! Eat at Zeke's! Eat at Zeke's!"

The sunset casts a beautiful glow over the crowd as the crescent moon blossoms to the east. For tonight, Detroit is lit up in an awesome orange and blue glow. The Nain Rouge hate could not push through, not this time.

As the crowd disperses in the early morning, Silvia smiles at the large pot of donations to rebuild Zeke's. She pulls out her cell phone and frowns as she erases a message from her young stalker. She smiles at a picture of her mother and father who sit as her screensaver. She proceeds to open a document she submitted in her creative writing class at college, "Eat@Zeke's, a family memoir." She received an A-.

EPILOGUE

Mama went home to join Ezekiel Sr. in the morning after the reunion. Her brief return coincided to bring her family back together. Her job was complete. The only remains of the former restaurant property are the large patio Zeke Sr. built with his bare hands. Mama's ashes are sprinkled by her reunited children in a new fountain propped in the middle of it. The water washes over newly planted flowers, herbs, and vegetables the family is growing to help sustain the business. Mama would be proud. Zeke Sr.'s old tree grows majestically in the far corner of the lot.

Her famous recipes were revealed in her last will and testament. To be shared among her children and their descendants long as the family business stayed intact.

Kwame made things right, marrying Ponyi and taking her and Kevin Jr. on the road with him and his band The Kommandoz. His boys often follow him on tour. He is cleared of all questioning stemming from his father's untimely passing. Kwame and Ezekiel get to know each other as brothers again.

Kayla took her portion of the divorce settlement and her share of the company to move back to Ohio. She stays in nearby Toledo, Ohio so that Matador and Kylie can be in driving distance from their father.

Maureen and Bailey were married among the ruins of Edgewater Park. They said it gave them an edge at the abandoned amusement park. They floated off into the lake on their very own Boblo boat. Maureen moved her advertising and marketing firm to Detroit. She joined in with the movement of 'Detroit Patented' to help bring the city back. Shinola watches are one of her biggest clients.

Silvia earned her degree in business and economics and uses their settlement and fundraiser money to help purchase a Food Truck. Zeke's lives on, rolling on wheels serving the core business it was built on, the manufacturing core and remaining inner-city neighborhoods of Detroit.

Bailey joins the staff of Zeke's Kitchen as the head cook. For a tatted up lil white girl from Illinois, she can throw down with healthy 'Soul Food'. Pook drives while Tanya, Sugar, and Moco serve customers. They add another lunch truck as Jaquan is finally hired permanently and they help him with a scholarship to attend Michigan University. His brother is well taken care of as the Woods take him in.

Ezekiel, does some serious soul searching and getting to re-know Utopia in another light, spending time with her, to know her as his daughter. He pays for her college tuition minus her earned scholarships. Ezekiel also takes accountability for his actions, serving at a neighborhood battered woman group giving his time and energy. The Vergeman's drop any charges against him as he continues doing right. He takes time to help paint and spruce up their meeting room at the community center under the guise of Freddy Styles. Freddy laments in joy as an anonymous donation to the center puts them in the financial black.

After Utopia leaves for school at Wilberforce University, Ezekiel reclaims his portion of Simon Woods Simon by suing his former partners for malpractice. He revamps the gentrification project for his old neighborhood, running Winkelman out of the equation. Winkelman was last seen filing for bankruptcy protection.

Instead of high priced condominiums, Ezekiel brings back affordable single-family homes to rebuild his old stomping grounds. With John George's help, they pass out building material and paint to all the owners of the remaining homes. The supplies help keeps them up with their new neighbors. The hood is evolving into a new neighborhood again without driving its long-time inhabitants away.

During all the activity, the original Zeke's Kitchen slowly gets rebuilt. The rebuilding of the original building is an ongoing task.

Under doctor's orders, Tyrone finally submits to giving up his favorite 'Soul Food' meal. All enablers have been summoned to cease assisting him. He is fit to be tied.

From above, Tyla and Ezekiel Woods Sr. look over their family and nod their heads in approval.

END

Deep Dish Meat and Collard Greens Pizza

Crust

¾ cup warm water (105° to 115°)
1 teaspoon active dry yeast
½ teaspoon sugar
¼ cup extra-virgin olive oil
2¼ cups all-purpose flour, divided
¼ cup plain cornmeal
½ teaspoon salt

Filling

4 teaspoons extra-virgin olive oil, divided
1 cup finely chopped onion
1 tablespoon minced fresh garlic
1-pound ground pork (or ground turkey)
3 cups chopped fresh collard greens
2 teaspoons fennel seed, crushed
½ teaspoon crushed red pepper
⅓ cup sun-dried tomatoes in oil, drained and chopped
2 teaspoons distilled white vinegar
1⅓ cups shredded smoked Cheddar cheese, divided
2 teaspoons plain cornmeal
1 cup shredded whole milk mozzarella cheese

For crust: In a large bowl, combine ¾ cup warm water, yeast, and sugar; let stand 5 minutes or until foamy. Add olive oil, 2 cups flour, cornmeal, and salt; stir until a soft dough forms.

Turn dough out onto a lightly floured surface. Knead until dough is smooth and elastic, approximately 6 minutes. (Add remaining ¼ cup flour, 2 teaspoons at a time, to keep dough from sticking.) Place dough in a medium bowl; spray top of dough with non-stick cooking spray. Cover, and let rise in a warm draft-free place (85°) until doubled in size, approximately 45 minutes.

For filling: In a large skillet, heat 2 teaspoons olive oil over medium-high heat. Add onion and garlic; cook 2 minutes, stirring frequently. Add meat; cook until browned and crumbly, approximately 7 minutes. Add collard greens, fennel seed, red pepper, tomatoes, and vinegar; cook 1 minute. Remove from heat. Stir in ⅓ cup Cheddar.

Preheat oven to 450°. Brush bottom only of a 10-inch (2-inch-deep) cast-iron skillet with remaining 2 teaspoons olive oil; sprinkle with cornmeal.

Lightly punch down dough. Cover, and let stand 5 minutes. On a lightly floured surface, roll dough into a 13-inch circle. Fold dough into quarters; place in prepared skillet. Unfold dough; lightly press into bottom and up sides of skillet. Add pork mixture; sprinkle with remaining 1 cup Cheddar and mozzarella.

Bake until golden brown, approximately 17 minutes. Let stand 5 minutes before serving.

Made in the USA
Monee, IL
18 August 2021